The Wife of Pilate
and Other Stories

GERTRUD VON LE FORT

The Wife of Pilate
and Other Stories

TRANSLATED BY
MICHAEL J. MILLER

IGNATIUS PRESS   SAN FRANCISCO

From the original German titles:
"Die Frau des Pilatus" © 1970,
"Plus Ultra" © 1950, and
"Am Tor des Himmels" © 1954 by
Insel Verlag, Frankfurt am Main and Leipzig

Cover design by John Herreid

ISBN 978-1-58617-639-6
Library of Congress Control Number 2014949953
Printed in the United States of America ∞

Contents

The Wife of Pilate

THE GREEK FREEDWOMAN Praxedis in Rome to Julia, the wife of Decius Gallicus in Vienna:

Honorable Lady, I just learned that in the next few days the Legion of Quintus Crassus is to be transferred from Rome to Gaul, and therefore I hasten to entrust to one of your tribunes the detailed report that your sisterly love for my dear mistress requested of me. For apparently in my first report I was unable to present things to you clearly enough. I beg you, pardon my confusion—when I wrote to you, I was still all too agitated by those deeply disturbing events. Moreover, there were doubts about the reliability of my messenger at that time, and the wave of persecution that is well known to you had still not completely died down. Meanwhile, the dangerous situation has improved. The messenger whom I have chosen now, though not one of your fellow believers, is taciturn and unprejudiced, a sober Roman who rejects that persecution with cool presence of mind, and so today I may confide in you frankly.

As you inform me, in Gaul nowadays they still tell the tale that the Procurator, after wandering in despair from place to place, sought and found death by a fall in the Swiss mountains. I need not correct this legend. You know that it is based on a fabrication: not the Procurator, but rather his wife, my beloved mistress Claudia Procula, wandered, as it were, through all the realms of this world —I say "as it were" because there are also spiritual realms that not only portend the world but in a higher sense *are* this real world. I begin, therefore, with that astonishing dream of my mistress, which you rightly suppose to be the root of her fate. I also agree with you completely when you distinguish between some dreams and others: there are in fact those that from the start bear the countenance of an imperative truth, even if no priest adept at auguring assures us of it. And while dreams usually flit past us as light-footed and swift as children playing hide-and-seek, the ones you mean stand before us from the start like the awe-inspiring statues at the Roman Forum, at the sight of which it is as though they were calling to the beholder: "Never forget us!" And the dream of which we are speaking was one of this latter sort, too.

I still remember very precisely all the circumstances that accompanied it, although several decades have passed since. My mistress, who was then still very young, was often melancholy in those days, because she felt neglected by her husband—you know, as a spoiled child she had a very demanding idea of a man's marital love. And it is true, the Procurator left her alone a lot in those days, but only due to the burden of the thousand troubles connected with the office he was obliged to hold among that small but extremely difficult people—duties that were, exceedingly irksome to his nature as a ruler. On the morning of which I am speaking, however, my mistress was all aglow with happiness and delight, for the Procurator had spent the whole night with her.

"O my Praxedis," she cried to me, "now Eros has favored me after all! Last night I was loved enough for my whole life." She directed her affectionate gaze toward the little statue of that charming god of love with which the Procurator had decorated her chamber. "No, I do not want to rise yet", she objected, as I prepared to help her dress. "Let me rest and dream a little more—in my mind I am still lying in my husband's arms." She allowed me to straighten her pillow for her and, smiling contentedly, nestled against it like a weary child.

Then while I was in the atrium arranging flowers and fruit for the table—I had sent the chattering slave girls out so that no one would disturb my mistress' slumber —I suddenly heard from the bedroom her fearful cry. As I entered her room, she was sitting on her couch, staring at me in wide-eyed bewilderment. The sweet satisfaction of happiness had been wiped off her childlike face, as though the shadow of many years yet to come had fallen over its youthful beauty or as though the inexorable fate appointed for her by the gods had met her in bodily form. She stretched out her arms to me, but immediately afterward allowed them to sink as though crippled: "Now all happiness for me is ended", she stammered. "I had such a bad dream, and surely you know, my Praxedis, that early morning dreams are prophetic!"

I asked her to tell me what she had seen in her dream, so that perhaps I might still be able to give it a good interpretation. Only gradually did she recover her fluent speech. "I found myself", she began, "in a shadowy room in which a multitude of people had gathered, who seemed to be praying, but their words just went past me like murmuring water. Suddenly, however, it was as though my ears were opened wide, or as if out of the muffled waters spurted the jet of a tall, rushing fountain—I heard with the utmost clarity the words: 'Suffered under Pontius Pilate, was crucified, died and was buried.' I could not figure out how my husband's name had come to be on the lips of these people or what it was supposed to mean; nevertheless I felt a vague dread of the words I had heard, as though they must have a mysteriously ominous meaning. Perplexed, I tried to leave the room, but then I found myself in another even darker one that reminded me of the cemetery outside the gates of Rome, which was filled with an even denser crowd of people praying than before—here, too, the startling words were pronounced: 'Suffered under Pontius Pilate, was crucified, died and was buried . . .' I tried to make my way out to the open air, but once more I arrived in an enclosed room, which this time had something sacred about it, and again I heard my husband's name from the mouths of the praying people who had gathered here, too. I hurried onward: room after room opened up ahead of me—at times I thought I recognized one of the temples in Rome that I know so well, but peculiarly changed: I saw marble ambos inlaid with gold and red precious stones, but not one of the familiar images of the gods. Often large, strange mosaics appeared in the apses, which seemed to depict an unknown god as a judge. But before I could get a good look at his face, the distressing words on the lips of a densely packed crowd sent shivers through me again: 'Suffered under Pontius Pilate, was crucified, died and was buried . . .' I ran farther and farther—citadel-like portals took me in, my feet hurried through immense, gravely solemn basilicas. The number of people assembled in them seemed to keep increasing, and the architecture became ever stranger—then suddenly the massive halls began to stand upright, as though they hovered weightlessly in the sky, freed from all the laws of stone. Here the assembled worshippers were silent, but invisible choirs sang, and from them, too, resounded the name of my husband: 'Crucifixus etiam pro nobis sub Pontio Pilato, passus et sepultus es . . .' Then the weightless halls vanished also, and familiar columns appeared, but adorned with strange draperies, the lofty splendor of which almost smothered them. Through the room supported by these columns streamed murmuring music: strange choirs whose many voices intertwined and parted again, so that the words floated into each other incomprehensibly. Suddenly, however, from the luxuriant waves of voices one arose: steep, stern, flawlessly clear, accusing, indeed, almost threatening, the words reechoed: 'Crucifixus etiam pro nobis sub Pontio Pilato . . .' I ran, I ran on as though pursued by Furies farther and still farther. It seemed to me as if I had hurried through centuries and had to hurry through still more centuries, as though until the end of all ages I was being hunted, persecuted by that most beloved name, as though it concealed an immensely heavy destiny that threatened to overshadow not only his dear life but also the life of all mankind . . .'' She stopped, for from outdoors we had heard for some time already an excited buzz of voices. Now the Procurator's name came to our ears also, and right afterward, as though in a mysterious variation of the voice just heard in the dream, the shouts of many voices resounded: "Crucify! Crucify him!"

Now, we knew the customs of that small, fanatical people among whom we were condemned to live, and we had grown accustomed to being treated from time to time to one of those ridiculous riots in the streets—that is, whenever the domineering priestly caste was intent on imposing its own capricious wishes on the Procurator. On other occasions we usually paid little attention to these endeavors. Today, however, it really looked to us as though something out there corresponded to the dream of my mistress that I had just heard—the distant centuries through which she believed she had hurried shrank back into the present moment, and this began to confirm my mistress' vision. A glance at her deathly pale face told me that she was thinking the same thing.

In order to calm her, I called one of the slave girls who were standing ready in the atrium, who always know all the news of the city, and asked her what was going on. She replied that the Jews had hauled a man before the courthouse, claiming that he was trying to make himself king and that the Procurator must have him crucified. They are indeed a wicked, ungrateful people, for this Jesus of Nazareth—that was the prisoner's name—had done much good for them; he was a great miracle worker and healer of the sick. She wanted to tell us still more, but I signaled for her to be quiet, for I noticed that the mistress became increasingly agitated at her account.

"Oh, I knew that morning dreams are prophetic", she exclaimed, when we were alone again. "Through this prisoner my dream will be fulfilled; the Procurator must not condemn him! Good Praxedis, go to him and ask him, in the name of all my tenderness, to set the accused man free. Hurry, for all the gods' sake, hurry!"

I hesitated, but not because I feared my errand. Our master was a courteous man; I will never forget the easy self-assurance with which he instantaneously declared me a freedwoman when he learned that I was Greek. It is just that in his official business he did not listen to women's voices—and I asked my mistress to consider that.

She persisted: "But today he will listen to mine, for last night he loved me."

So I put away my misgivings and went over to that part of the palace which they call the courthouse. The centurion on duty brought me into the presence of the Procurator. Although he was much older than his wife, he looked very youthful that morning with his imposing stature, powerful chin, and narrow, tight-lipped mouth. Having just come from the bath and clothed in a fresh toga, he was about to go out to the tumultuous crowd —it is indeed one of the countless oddities of the Jews that they think they become impure if they set foot in our houses.

I presented my message—he listened to me with calm self-restraint; nothing in his facial expression indicated that he was in a hurry. I think if I had spoken a half hour, he would not have interrupted me; indeed, it actually seemed to me as though it were quite all right with him to keep the unruly people outside waiting. (You know, my lady, that he could often be spiteful toward them in this wordless way.)

"Very good, Praxedis, I thank your mistress; give her my greetings", he finally said, and although his face—ah, these inscrutable Roman faces!—betrayed to me nothing of what he thought about my message, I had the distinct impression that it was not unwelcome to him, almost as though it corroborated his own opinion of the prisoner.

Now I hurried back to my mistress and notified her that the Procurator had listened to me benevolently. That seemed to calm her somewhat. She allowed me to dress her and also applied extensively the many cosmetics and ointments by which she set great store, notwithstanding her youthful freshness. Then we went over to the *triclinium*, the dining room, where we could not hear the ongoing uproar of the people. I read several Greek love poems aloud to her, which she was especially fond of hearing because they reflected the feelings she was accustomed to demanding of her husband.

Suddenly the slave girl whom I had questioned previously on account of the riot burst in. "O my lady, your husband is allowing the prisoner to be crucified after all," she cried, "and his friends firmly believed that God's angels would come to his aid." My mistress jumped up and literally fled the room. I followed her but could not catch up with her. Then we two were standing on the flat roof above the low porch of the palace, from which one has a view of the whole square at the foot of the courthouse. We leaned over the wall.

The Procurator now sat on the judge's bench, glaring ominously; evidently he had already pronounced the sentence, for the legionaries were laying hands on the prisoner who stood before him. He was clothed in a ragged red military cloak and wore a crown of thorns around his bleeding head. But the truly distressing thing about his appearance was that this pitiful being looked as though he had pity on the whole world, even on the Procurator, his judge—yes, even on him! This pity engulfed the entire face of the condemned man—and if my life depended on it, I could not say the slightest thing about it except that he wore this expression of an unbounded, perfectly incomprehensible pity, at the sight of which I was seized by a peculiar vertigo. It seemed to me as though this pity would necessarily engulf the whole known world, just as it had engulfed the prisoner's face to the point where he was unrecognizable. Indeed, the impression that the whole world as I knew it had somehow begun to totter was so overwhelming that, despite its all-powerful influence, it aroused my opposition. I felt a hopeless resistance abruptly rise up within me; I clung to my condemned world and persisted in this attitude, motionless, albeit helpless. All this took place in an instant, and in the next the legionaries were already roughly dragging the condemned man away so as to lead him to his crucifixion. The Procurator stood up from the tribunal and went back into the palace with the same ominous expression.

What had happened? Whence this changed attitude? We later learned that the bloodthirsty mob had reproached him for harming the Emperor's interests if he did not accede to their wishes. Yes, noble Julia, I know that your fellow believers therefore accuse him of selfish ambition, yet that judgment may be rather superficial. Certainly the Procurator handed over an innocent man, and he knew it.

But has Rome ever hesitated to abandon innocent men when the tranquility of the Empire was at stake somewhere? The whole situation in the East was extremely tense at that time—any Roman would probably have acted as the Procurator did. Then too: What is the life of a single man worth to a Roman? And our master was a Roman from head to foot. Moreover, he belonged to that later generation which still sacrificed to the gods only out of a certain courtesy toward their ancestors—for him there was ultimately only one sanctuary and one place of sacrifice: the Roman Empire of the deified Caesar.

I now asked leave of my mistress to bring her back to her chambers. She stood as if struck by lightning, shattered, as though she herself and not that Jewish man had been condemned to death. As I spoke to her, she placed her hands in front of her face and wept a long time, fervently and hopelessly, yet in utter silence. She remained silent, too, when in the course of that day a remarkable, completely inexplicable darkness spread over the land, and while everyone else in the palace was running to and fro anxiously, she seemed to nestle into that darkness as though into something that profoundly matched her own feelings. Even later she never spoke about what had happened on that day, which gradually began to astonish me, for her custom had been to unload all her feelings and experiences onto me, as a child might do. For the first time I was confronting her reticence, and so for a long time I did not grasp the fact that the glance of that condemned innocent man had wounded and transformed her forever. And yet that glance had not fallen upon her personally: it had been directed exclusively at her husband, but precisely for that reason it had hit her, and now it became evident what her hitherto so childishly selfish love was capable of. Today I know that she then took his guilt upon herself, by no means consciously or through a deliberate decision, but simply as the emanation of a love that had burst through its previous boundaries. Henceforth she was sad, while he enjoyed life; she suffered, while he apparently felt content, and finally she even endured his estrangement from her because he no longer understood her. I began to suspect her total transformation when the child she had conceived in that night of love came into the world dead without any outburst of lamentation from her. Frankly, it was as if she were inwardly prepared for that blow, as previously for the darkening of nature, and put up with it patiently, albeit mournfully. To console her, I remarked that at her youthful age she could still hope for many children, but she seemed not to hear, and in fact she never had the privilege of expecting a second child, although she welcomed her husband now as before with great tenderness. But now she waited without impatience when he did not come to her chamber, and there was a tender, very quiet resignation in her embrace, often something like pain. When she looked at him with her big, innocent eyes, I sometimes unexpectedly had to think of his unjust sentence, and I found myself tempted for a moment to believe that the image of that condemned man was trying to force itself between these two people. That could not be, however, if only because the Procurator obviously thought no more about that incident.

When he was then called back to Rome shortly thereafter, his memories of Judaea seemed to sink into the depths of the sea. The Emperor at that time showered him with honorary commissions, and he was content to have the benefit of these distinctions. My mistress, too, was well received in Rome, as befitted her rank and her husband's position, but curiously Rome was no longer well received by her. Although in Jerusalem she had always longed to return there, now it almost appeared as if she were longing to go back to Jerusalem. The noisy festivals of the metropolis, which had once enchanted her, repelled her. Her eyes filled with tears when she heard of the mistreatment of a slave. During the triumphal processions of victorious generals, in which the whole populace participated exultantly, she trembled at the fate of the captured barbarian princes, who were customarily killed on the Capitol once the triumph was over. She had a particular horror, though, of the public games: the dying gladiators—indeed, even the wild animals that were pitted against one another to entertain the people—caused her pain and torment. She shivered whenever she had to accompany her husband to the circus.

He at that time had become particularly fond of the magnificent spectacle of the chariot races. He had the ambition of driving a *quadriga,* a chariot drawn by four horses, himself and sacrificed for this ambition by spending whole days in the hot baths and by performing all sorts of exercises, which were supposed to counteract his tendency to corpulence and to help him lose weight. Indeed, in his ambition he went so far as to have his favorite slave instructed in the weird magical arts of one of those sorcerers who were said to be able to obtain victories in the circus through certain outrageously cruel sacrifices to the demons. Now this was an odd concession for the enlightened mind of our master—I myself could not suppress a smile at this contradiction, and I thought I glimpsed one on the face of the cunning slave, too—but Claudia did not smile when she heard about it; it only increased her dread of the games.

The Procurator shook his head at her horror. "You will nevertheless rejoice over my victory," he said confidently, "and they will rejoice over you—the people will exultantly surround the victor's beautiful wife, my Claudia will celebrate triumphs that far surpass my own . . ." He stopped, surprised that this homage no longer flattered her. "Can you really have forgotten how beautiful you are?" he asked in astonishment. But this appeal, too, faded away without any effect.

"I fear for you", she said softly.

"Fear when I drive the *quadriga*?" he snapped indignantly.

She replied, "Not only when you drive the *quadriga* . . ." Now he looked at her with a peculiar anxiety. For a few seconds it was as though the two were about to engage in a conversation that was long overdue yet had never come to pass. But already the Procurator turned away with a strangely vehement gesture, as though he could not bear the sight of her.

Later on I repeatedly had the impression that he became impatient, irritated by her concern for him—no doubt he had found the egotistical little coquette of yesteryear much more attractive. And yet at that time, Claudia's beauty had just fully unfolded. But strangely enough, she no longer had an effect on him; her eyes, especially, which he had marveled at earlier, left him cold—no, more than that: sometimes it was as if they caused him uneasiness. Claudia's beauty no longer impressed society, either. Perhaps it was because she now neglected the stylish cosmetics that formerly charmed the world. I conscientiously brought her the little paint pots and the beauty creams, and she was also quite willing to use them, but again and again she forgot to do so if I did not remind her.

"She is governed by the strict customs of our ancestors; she has no relationship to the living Rome", society grumbled when she appeared trembling and pale beside her husband at the circus, her soul increasingly transparent through her face.

At any rate there was no denying now that this living Rome was a new reality with which one had to make friends or to which one had to resign oneself. Back at the time we set out for Judaea, the successor of the great Augustus was still reigning and the resplendence of his name filled everyone with pride and confidence. That resplendence was of course extinguished now: terrible death sentences had darkened the final years of Tiberius. In vain did people look in the Senate for men who bore many familiar names. The Roman aristocracy had learned to die, but those who were spared knew how to live. It was almost as though the horror they had gone through procured for them an easier, less troubled existence. In fact, no one in Rome spoke any more about those sinister events; the honorable dead, those victims of the criminal authorities, seemed to be forgotten. Amusing tales of scandal, dubious amorous adventures, and above all the successes in the arena occupied minds, and everyone seemed to be content with that. Even the Procurator was no exception. "Men, after all, are fleeting, but the Empire is eternal", he used to say when occasionally someone did speak about those dead aristocrats.

Only once did I see him momentarily alarmed, when one of his freedmen told him with a sneering smile how in the final days of the deceased Emperor one could hear everywhere in Rome the shout: "Into the Tiber with Tiberius!" Now, it was a very similar shout we had once heard in Jerusalem, but I hardly think the Procurator gave this comparison any thought—if it occurred to him at all. Besides, how could he subject the Roman Empire, which to him was the greatest thing of all, to such a comparison? And yet this comparison was all too obvious. At that time there were already new reports of horrific murders in the imperial household and in the city. But although the Procurator had shut his eyes to the crimes of old Tiberius, now he seemed to consider it his duty to defend outright the insane acts of young Caligula.

"The welfare of the Empire, after all, sometimes demands unjust sacrifices", he used to say to his wife—I could not help thinking that it sounded almost as though he were defending himself.

"The welfare of the Empire demands unjust sacrifices", she repeated flatly—once again that conversation which had never taken place seemed to be hovering in the air.

"What do you mean? You were going to say something . . .", he asked insecurely. She crossed her arms over her bosom fleetingly, then suddenly decided to take his right hand and gently caressed it.

"Do you know, back then . . .", she began, looking at him wide-eyed.

"No, I no longer know anything", he interrupted her, turning away severely. "Thanks be to the gods, I no longer need to know anything about Jerusalem!" What brought up Jerusalem? My mistress had not said a single word about the city—or had I not heard her mention its name?

In such moments, which were already familiar to me, I always had the compelling sense that her love was trying to summon him to reflect on something, although it was uncertain whether he still could reflect on it. She then resembled someone who feels obliged to awaken a sleeper and yet recoils from disturbing his rest. He had some inkling of this process. One moment it was as though he were walking quickly and unsuspectingly toward a door he was supposed to open, but before he reached it he decisively turned around in bewilderment. This process repeated itself many times. I had the feeling then that inwardly he was slowly turning away from his wife.

The years passed now without any apparent change in the relationship between the two spouses. I do not know whether I grew accustomed to the tension between them or whether it receded over time—in any case, there was no more talk about Jerusalem. That oft-postponed conversation had still not taken place, but no one was expecting it any more, either. The Procurator was already an aging man now. Beneath his strong, chiseled chin, a little cushion of fat had formed, and the daily hot baths could no longer reduce his increasing body weight. Like most Roman men, he had gone prematurely bald, which is why, following the example of the great Caesar, he liked to appear in public wearing a wreath of ivy or vine leaves. Claudia, too, who was many years younger, had faded, but a tender expression of searching expectation still gave her animated face a hint of youth. Over the years, the Procurator had withdrawn more and more from her; his name was often mentioned in relation to other women. She knew this and endured it, as she had once endured the death of her child, but I do not think he ever stopped loving her. Indeed, often I had the odd impression that something seemingly divisive united them deeply. Many people were surprised that he did not dissolve his marriage with Claudia, since now as before she remained childless; some even wondered why Claudia herself did not insist on the divorce and remarriage of her husband, so as to allow him the belated happiness of descendants. But as far as I know, this idea was never considered—a surprising fact, no doubt, even if you recall that the marriage of those two people was one of the last to be contracted in the old sacral form in the presence of the *pontifex maximus* with a joint sacrifice in the Temple of Capitoline Jupiter. But as early as the latter years of Tiberius, even marriages of that sort were no longer indissoluble, and during the reigns of Caligula and Nero, who still felt bound by the old gods? With the passage of years, Claudia, too, had increasingly turned away from the deities to which she had once clung with childlike trust. One might think that she had been infected by her husband's skepticism, and yet there was a world of difference: the Procurator's godlessness did not trouble him in the least, while Claudia found it the source of a deep uneasiness, as often happens to people who see their years slipping away without the fulfillment of what they had really expected out of life.

I still remember how I once accompanied her in her sedan chair across the Forum. It was a brilliant spring morning, the temples and palaces were literally bathed in light, and never had the primordial sun shone on anything so proud and lordly. You know, noble Julia, that I am otherwise rather reserved in my opinion of Roman edifices —in my homeland, buildings were simpler and therefore, it seems to me, nobler—but on that morning, at the sight of that white marble splendor, I could not help thinking of sea foam: just as the goddess Aphrodite emerged from the latter, so it appeared to me that the goddess Roma stood up out of the former. I said this to my mistress, but she shook her head brusquely. It seemed to me as though a strangely opaque veil lay over her eyes—was the transformation of Rome that was clear to me not the only one that had occurred in her eyes? Was there in this city still an unknown cell in which mysterious atmospheric conditions were brewing, something quiet and powerful that had not existed before?

At that time, my mistress began to turn to those new cults which the foreign tradesmen and legionaries brought with them into the metropolis. We visited the Temple of Cybele; I had to accompany her to the mysteries of the Egyptian Isis and to those of the Syrian goddess, of Adonis and of the Great Mother. But even though she devoted herself with great fervor to each of these deities to begin with, again and again it was as if she had intended to find a completely different one, and she turned away, disappointed, to search once more. Finally, she asked to be brought to the famous Sybil of Tibur in order to learn the name of that deity whom the latter notoriously had foretold to the great Augustus.—Surely you still recall, noble Julia, the saying of the Sybil that used to circulate years ago among the people everywhere: "From heaven comes the king of the ages."

And so we traveled to Tibur [modern Tivoli]. The Sybil was an ancient woman who seemed not to notice us at all when we stepped into the famous grotto. She sat with her eyes closed in front of her hearth, on which the fire seemed to be extinguished like the light in the old woman's face. It was dark in the grotto, as though it were the entrance to the fields of the underworld. When I spoke to the Sybil, she made no answer—probably she did not hear me, for the rushing of the nearby waterfalls filled the space, as though nature were trying to engulf the human voice. Then, however, my mistress wordlessly touched the shoulder of the sunken figure, and the latter lifted her heavy head—the coals on the fireplace abruptly burst into flames again, and now it was as if two sisterly creatures recognized each other. Wide-eyed, the ancient woman straightened up and stroked my mistress' forehead and eyes with her spectral, trembling hand.

"Yes, I know, you too have seen him", she murmured. "What do you want from me, then? My time is over." But then suddenly her eyes became pale, as though struck by a strange light: it appeared as if her own sight were being taken from her. Foam appeared at her lips, as happened whenever she prophesied. She cried in an almost painfully loud voice: "Go to the Subura, to the poorest house you find—there is someone who knows more than

I . . ." And then once again, sighing profoundly and contentedly: "My time is over—my world is gone . . ."

Now, you can imagine, noble Julia, that I was not prepared to take an evening stroll in the Subura, that rather infamous district where the insignificant people make their purchases and timid poverty dwells, sometimes along with insolent depravity, in high tenement houses. But my mistress could not be talked out of the Subura, especially since she had heard from one of our slave girls about a new kind of worship that was supposed to take place at an evening hour inside a house in that dismal quarter.

We entered a miserable room that by day may have served as the workshop of some petty artisan; now a number of people were assembling in it. The slave girl who had given us directions to the place had also told us the password. Upon saying it, we were trustfully admitted, but I persuaded my mistress to stay in the background, for the character of the little assembly seemed rather sinister to me. These were the poorest of the poor, among them many slaves and also, unmistakably, several prostitutes; these sorts of people, though, are prone to outbursts against high-ranking individuals, if they know they outnumber them. After a while, an old man in worn-out traveler's garb entered and knelt down in front of a simple table that had been festively arranged: it was an altar, and yet we could see no preparations whatsoever for the offering of a sacrificial animal. The old man recited a prayer, of which we understood very little on account of his strange accent. Then he stood up and invited those present to recite together the profession of their faith.

And now something completely unexpected happened. Those present had stood up at the bidding of the old man—evidently the priest of this worshipping community. Timidly, obviously unused to choral speaking, they complied. They, too, used our language with many barbarian accents, so that at first we caught nothing coherent. Suddenly I sensed that beside me Claudia Procula began to tremble violently—I shuddered at a heavy feeling that this miserable, dimly lit room with its murmuring assembly was the unearthly repetition of something I had long since forgotten. Immediately thereafter, as though it had been breathlessly catapulted up out of oblivion, I was overcome by the memory of that strange dream that my mistress had had back then in Jerusalem. Suddenly my hearing was miraculously acute, and now I too heard the words: "Suffered under Pontius Pilate, was crucified, died and was buried . . ."

Please do not ask me, noble Julia, to describe the effect these words had on my mistress. She stood, as once on the balcony of the courthouse in Jerusalem, as though struck by lightning. But as I put my arms around her and gently tried to lead her out, she abruptly tore herself away from me and impetuously pressed through the crowd toward the front. The praying choir had now fallen silent, and the old traveling preacher began to speak: "I continue to proclaim to you the history of our Lord's Passion. We are drawing near to its climax. The hearing before the Roman procurator is over. I am now following the report of our brother in Jerusalem who was an eyewitness, and in your presence I testify to the event with his words: '. . . And Pilate sat down on the judgment seat at a place called The Pavement, and in Hebrew, Gabbatha. Now it was the day of Preparation of the Passover; it was about the sixth hour . . .' "

You know, honorable Julia, that after that we frequently, indeed very soon regularly, took part in the assemblies of the Nazarenes—that was what I called the members of that little congregation in the Subura—and that my mistress very soon and very fervently accepted their message, while I, at the proclamation of the Crucified One, yearned for the beautiful, serene gods of my native Greece. I tried also to persuade my mistress by asking her to reflect: If the condemned man really were one of the heavenly beings, he could have saved himself from the snare of his enemies. She replied softly but firmly: "But he was one of the heavenly beings, for he regarded his unjust judge with mercy." Then I could not contradict her, since that look of compassion had made an impression on me, too, like a greeting from another world entirely, and I felt that this complete otherness was what my mistress had been seeking in vain before and now had finally found.

And yet her discovery was accompanied by new, profound sorrow. She had grown accustomed to her own cultic gesture that expressed this sorrow: she could never listen to the creed of the Nazarenes without covering her head at the name Pontius Pilate, just as she never dared, despite all her devotion to her new faith, to request baptism, the actual initiation into the community. She feared that they would loathe her if she announced that she was the wife of Pontius Pilate, and I did not dare to relieve her of what seemed to me a justified fear. So then we two attended these assemblies as nameless figures, although that seemed to disturb no one. The greeting, "*Marana tha*, Come, Lord", was enough to make this friendly, unsuspecting community tolerate our presence in its midst.

Nevertheless, even these simple people were struck by the reticence and grief of my mistress. After the old traveling preacher went away, the community was led by his young assistant. Whenever he invited newcomers to prepare for baptism, he looked expectantly at my mistress, but she had already veiled her head with a sorrowful gesture.

Sometimes on the way home, several participants in the assembly joined us. They trustingly poured out their hearts to us, which, to our astonishment, burned not only with expectation for the next world but also with a great hope for this life.

There was an old Syrian woman with features that were once beautiful but now completely ravaged. She claimed to know that the downfall of the unbelieving world would take place very soon. Then the horrible circus games would come to an end, the wild animals would come out of their cages and nestle at the feet of the humans, and the gladiators would throw their swords away. The rich would distribute their goods, the masters would set their slaves free, and over the Palatine of the cruel Caesars the Holy Spirit would appear as a dove. "*Marana tha, Marana tha*, Come, Lord!" she cried, "so believe it, all of you, rejoice, all of you!" Then, to my mistress, who was walking silently beside her: "And you, poor, sorrowful sister, you will then be as happy as a young, radiant bride! *Marana tha*, Come, Lord!"

Only the Lord did not come; what came was bloody persecution. You know, noble Julia, about the unfortunate conflagration at that time that reduced several districts of the poorer population of Rome to rubble and ashes, for which innocent people were then held responsible in order to calm the embittered populace. One evening, when we again tried to enter the gloomy old tenement house in the Subura, we were stopped at the door for the first time, and they asked our names. My mistress hesitated even now to mention it. But it became evident that suddenly a new and completely different mood prevailed in the community. In a flash we were surrounded by frightened people who stared at us suspiciously.

"What is your name? Why do you not tell us who you are?" we heard on every side. And then, as though in gnawing fear: "You do not bother to prepare for baptism —what do you want from us, then?"

Now the old Syrian woman made her way through the crowd: "Calm down, calm down, dear friends," she cried imploringly, "the Lord will come and protect us— do not worry, then: all the hairs on our heads have been counted—the one who said that will not abandon us— *Marana tha*, Come, Lord!"

But then a man's rough voice snapped at her: "Keep quiet, you old witch! For a long time the Lord has not come, but danger is coming!" Then, addressing Claudia: "Not one step farther until we know who you are and what you want from us!" The speaker, a gigantic

Ethiopian slave, stood in front of my mistress with his feet wide apart and blocked the entrance to the house. My mistress had gone deathly pale, but she remained silent— the aristocratic Roman matron did not allow herself to be intimidated.

Meanwhile, the commotion had steadily increased. The Ethiopian had grabbed my mistress by the shoulders and was shaking her. "I want to know your name. Your name, you haughty creature!"

At that terribly distressing moment, the Apostle's young assistant appeared. "What is going on here?" he cried imperiously.

The Ethiopian answered defiantly: "What is going on here is what you ordered. We asked an unknown woman her name, but she will not give it!"

The assistant, an earnest, still young Roman, ordered the crowd to be calm. Then, turning to the Ethiopian, he said: "Let the woman go!" and to her, "What is your name? Say your name."

She replied, "I will gladly say it, but only to you alone."

He silently brought us into a small adjoining room. "Forgive the commotion", he said in a friendly tone. "Rumors are circulating in the city, which hopefully will not be confirmed, but these people feel threatened—their frailty is great, and you never asked for baptism. Until now we have not asked you why, but today it becomes necessary. We are afraid that someone is spying on us."

"Sir, I would gladly have asked for baptism," she said simply, "but I did not dare to say my name, for I feared that it would frighten you—I am Claudia Procula—the wife of Pontius Pilate."

Hearing the Procurator's name, the surprised assistant flinched, but immediately afterward something like joy appeared in his face. "Your name does not frighten us, Claudia Procula", he replied. "The disciple of the Lord whom you heard preaching assured us that you warned your husband not to pass an unjust judgment. You have no share in his guilt and can hold your head high and uncovered when we recite the profession of faith . . ."

She replied, "Sir, allow me to continue covering my head; it is hard for me to hear this profession, for I am profoundly united with my husband. Can I not do penance for him, so that his name might be stricken from the creed?"

The young Roman regarded her earnestly. "No, Claudia Procula," he said solemnly, "you cannot. Whenever this profession of faith is recited, the name Pontius Pilate will also be pronounced. With that name your husband once stood for the Roman Empire in Jerusalem, and therefore he now stands for all time to testify to the place and hour of the event."

On her face appeared once again that animated, sorrowful expression. "And yet," she said fervently, "our Lord meant him, too, when he prayed: 'Father, forgive them, for they know not what they do.'"

"But your husband knew what he was doing—you yourself told him", replied the assistant with some severity.

"But he did not understand me," she begged, "he did not recognize God's mercy in the accused man—how could he recognize it?—there is no mercy in his world!"

"Nevertheless, he knew that he was handing an innocent man over to death", the assistant continued. "Poor woman, there is nothing consoling that I can tell you: your husband is condemned, since he condemned the Lord— and you do not believe aright if you dispute God's justice. Allow yourself to be instructed in the faith, and you will understand it."

She was silent for a while, during which her placid face slowly assumed an unyielding expression. Finally she said softly and solemnly: "Farewell. I was not seeking God's justice here; I sought Christ's mercy—which is not of this world but something entirely different—yet you are just as unfamiliar with it as my husband was. He was not the only one guilty of the Lord's death; all of you were, too. And at this moment you are guilty of it again, be-cause you are abandoning his divine mercy!"

The young assistant seemed disconcerted for a mo-ment. But then immediately his features hardened into a frightening judicial expression. "What do you know, woman, about God's justice? Are you trying to teach us, although you are not even baptized and can never be bap-tized if you insist on your error? Go now and think about what I said." Once again he opened a side door and let us out, unnoticed by the crowd.

The night was very dark, and restless clouds hurried past the moon. Through the gloomy streets the glow of a torch wandered from time to time, carried by the out-rider at the head of a nocturnal cavalcade. It cast its flick-ering light on the dismal houses of the Subura, so an-cient that they were long since ready for demolition, yet crammed with people living according to centuries-old customs, sinning, and finally dying, so as to make room for others, who in turn lived according to the same dull, monotonous customs, sinned, and died. Now and then one could hear from a distant amphitheater the roaring of the wild animals or the signals of the praetorians out of a barracks. Prostitutes flitted past us, laughing impudently.

My mistress walked extremely fast, as if she could not leave the Subura quickly enough. I knew that she was wretched, but I did not dare say a word to console her —I felt her disappointment as if it were my own. So we reached the district of the Imperial Forums. The moon had now emerged from the clouds—the Palatine loomed marble-white before our eyes. Along the street on which we were walking, one temple followed another in a series—the fortresses of the old gods. At one point, the division of a marching legion overtook us: the uniform step of their feet shook the night like the iron rhythm of Rome.

Now we were walking along the high temple wall of Mars Ultor. Suddenly my mistress stopped and touched the cold wall with one uplifted hand.

"Mars Ultor," she said softly, "Mars, the Avenger! Oh, how firm your house stands—and I was foolish enough to believe that it was falling! But it will never fall—the Nazarenes will not topple it, either—again and again Caesar will be victorious over Christ, as he once conquered Christ in Jerusalem. Again and again they will kill the captured barbarian princes on the Capitol and offer to the gods the bloody sacrifices of innocent animals—again and again our legions will crush peaceful peoples—again and again they will say: Woe to the conquered! Again and again they will shout: An eye for an eye, a tooth for a tooth! And if Christ were to come again today, as the Syrian woman expected, even then nothing would change—they would once again nail him to the cross, and everything would remain as it is—the Absolutely Other does not come; instead, the same thing always comes in this world and will come eternally. And if the Nazarenes really were to win this city and every temple of the old gods were consecrated to Christ—this city would nevertheless remain what it is, not the city of Christ, but the city of Caesar . . ."

"But perhaps", I ventured to object, "Christ would look at this city as he once looked at his judge . . ."

She gave no answer—I did not know whether she had not heard me or whether she did not want to hear me.

From then on we no longer went to the assemblies of the Nazarenes, and although I saw how much this break pained my mistress, I was nevertheless glad, because in Rome accusations against the little community were making the rounds in ever wider circles. The Procurator, too, found himself forced then for the first time to take note of that community. He was suffering as a result of a recent shoulder injury, which he had incurred by a fall during one of those chariot races which long since were beyond the stamina of a man of his age.

But as you know, noble Julia, one of the wicked amusements of the young Emperor Nero was to force even white-haired senators into the arena and to make fun of their clumsiness. The Procurator was all the more unhappy about his defeat because he already feared that he had fallen into disfavor on the Palatine—for quite some time now they had no longer employed his services there.

The doctor called on him every day to bandage him; before hurrying on to the next house, he would pause to relate a lot of news that was meant to distract the patient from his condition. So he, too, heard one day that they were blaming a certain sect called the "Nazarenes" for the conflagration in Rome.

"Of course I consider them completely harmless", said the doctor. "Imagine, Pontius Pilate, they believe in a certain Jesus of Nazareth, whom they have divinized in a way modeled on our imperial cult. The man in question was a young visionary who around thirty years ago was crucified in Jerusalem because he made himself out to be the Messiah of the Jews. Actually you ought to know more details about him, because you must have been there then, when you were Procurator in Judaea . . ."

The Procurator, bored, shrugged his shoulders—the time when the memory of Judaea still bothered him was past. Not one muscle moved on his aristocratic Roman face—only the little pillow of fat under his chin, which he was so unhappy about, rose and sank a bit as a result of his shortness of breath.

"Really, I no longer remember, my friend", he replied distractedly. "Those Jewish affairs were always very unpleasant, and I usually do not think about them anymore."

"Too bad", said the talkative doctor, who probably had hoped to learn from the Procurator more about the origin of the Nazarenes. He turned to Claudia: "Does my lady remember nothing more, either?" As usual, she and I were in the room, helping the doctor bandage the wound—the Procurator insisted on Claudia's presence;

generally, since he had been suffering, he seemed to feel that her closeness was a silent good deed.

When the doctor spoke to her, the instrument suddenly fell out of her hand. I picked it up and tried to give it to her, but she did not notice it; she was aghast.

"Oh, yes", she stammered. "Oh, yes, I remember. It was back then when I dreamed . . ." She hesitated. I too held my breath: the discussion that had never had its due and had long since been buried in silence suddenly stood in the room, inescapably close. But strangely, the Procurator did not notice it—or should I say: no longer noticed? Had it actually become too late for him to remember?

"What sort of a dream was it?" he asked guilelessly.

"The dream was a premonition", she stammered.

"And of course I heeded your warning?" he said good-naturedly . . .

"No, you pronounced the sentence anyway . . ." She stopped short. Obviously she felt inhibited by the doctor's presence. But now he joined in again.

"Did my lady's premonition perhaps concern that crucified man?" he asked. "Then you would in fact have been the one who sentenced him, Pontius Pilate. I thought so right away—the period of time points too clearly to it. Don't you remember it now . . . ?"

The Procurator looked down at his hands distractedly—during the bandaging of his shoulder a few drops of blood had fallen on them. I handed him a bowl of scented water, and he dipped his hands into it. Suddenly he flinched: "Ah, yes, I remember dimly", he said. "The

Jews once brought me a man who took himself to be their Messiah—and, by Capitoline Jupiter, that man had a strange look! Never before or afterward has anyone looked at me that way . . ." He suddenly stopped short, evading his wife's gaze. A short, completely impenetrable silence ensued—then the discussion went on, seemingly uninterrupted.

"So they are trying to blame these Nazarenes for the catastrophic fire in Rome?" the Procurator asked, turning again to the doctor. "What a misguided idea! But of course something must be done to pacify the people."

"Yes, of course", the doctor agreed. "And they have already executed several of these Nazarenes. They are said to have died very steadfastly, professing their faith to the last and even forgiving their executioners. But what is the matter with my lady?" he interrupted himself, jumping up. "May I assist you, Claudia Procula?"

She made no reply but hurried out, reeling. I followed her. Outside she threw herself into my arms, sobbing.

"And I condemned these people, just as they condemned my husband and as my husband once condemned the Lord! In the same way! But Christ set up his sign over them—he made them his witnesses, even to the shedding of their blood! Yes, truly, Christ is always and everywhere defeated, and he was defeated in me, too—they were right to refuse me baptism, oh, they were right!"

Meanwhile the Procurator was impatiently striking the gong with the little metal ball. I went in to him to reassure him about his wife's fainting spell. Well, he was accustomed to her impulsive emotions and seemed to give no more thought to the outcome of the discussion. But after only a few days he was reminded of it again. An imperial command arrived that, under the pretext of revealing the causes of the catastrophic fire in Rome, put him in charge of striking a blow against the Nazarenes. I thought that Claudia would be horrified, but the opposite occurred.

"God is very gracious—God is very gracious", she said with emotion when she learned about the imperial command. "He is giving my husband a second chance to make the right decision." Then she sent me to him to invite him to her chamber. I found him in a very good mood: on the previous day the doctor had removed his sling, he felt restored to health, and the Emperor's command had relieved him of the fear that he had fallen into disfavor. The slave whom he had once sent for instructions in the magical arts was with him. After his fall during a chariot race, the Procurator had banished him from his society. I was surprised to find him there again, that mysterious man, whose sly, enigmatic face seemed to me today to be strikingly sinister.

The Procurator, as always, listened to me politely. But then he replied that his wife could expect him in the atrium instead of in her chamber. It was clear to me right away that he was guided by a wish directly opposed to hers. Claudia was concerned with being alone with him, while he had avoided that since the discussion in the doctor's presence.

I then returned to my mistress, and we walked together over to the atrium. The morning sun fell into the open space, the colonnade lay in the shadows, as well as the little temple with the ancient household gods, but the marble bench beside the basin of the fountain, where my mistress sat down, lay in the warm sunlight. In this peaceful corner, the tumult of the people from distant streets was muted, but stronger than on other days.

It took a rather long time for the Procurator to appear. The sedan chair that was to bring him to the Palatine was expected at any moment. The slave appointed to serve him already stood by the luggage under the columns, which made it possible for him to overhear our discussion. Other domestics, too, continually scurried past on business. But the Procurator had counted on this semipublic setting; he even detained me when I started to leave. But he was disappointed: none of this mattered to Claudia; she did not even notice it; she was too deeply preoccupied by the importance of this hour that she had hoped and waited for year after year. Now it did not even occur to this sensitive, boundlessly taciturn woman that she was not alone with her husband.

She calmly accepted his parting words, but then she came straight to the point. Very softly, but very firmly she said: "I beseech you, my husband, give the commission back to the Emperor. Have nothing to do with the persecution of these Nazarenes; do not get involved once again with the condemnation of innocence." In a single instant the whole situation was now clear in its distressing repetition. The Procurator seemed unsurprised by Claudia's unusual petition.

"Truly, I have nothing against these little sects", he said calmly. "What do I care about the Nazarenes? For a Roman it is always a question of Rome only, and Rome is the imperial will. The Palatine informed me that these people are arsonists. Moreover, if they should fail to offer due sacrifice to the Emperor, they are to be regarded as insurgents as well."

"They are no more insurrectionists than was the man after whom they are named", she replied, still with the same imperturbable meekness.

He understood right away what she meant. "Nevertheless," he said, "he was suspected of trying to make himself king. Indeed, he himself admitted it to me."

"But his kingdom is not of this world", she countered.

"He said that, too, at the time, but what was I supposed to think? A kingdom that is not of this world—who ever heard of such a kingdom?"

"Someone who is of the truth." Did Claudia's voice say that?—How strange this almost verbatim repetition!

The Procurator shrugged his shoulders. "What is truth? Our philosophers would be happy if they could tell us. Maybe you know more than they?"

"I know that you did not know who it was that you condemned." Her voice now had the utmost tenderness. "Yes, he was and is a king: the king of the ages whom the Sybil of Tibur foretold to Augustus."

Now it was as though he were abruptly seized with dread—the last dam broke: the never-forgotten, unforgettable act rushed out of the depths. "How can you say", he shouted, "that I condemned him? The Jews forced me to hand him over—I defended his innocence to the last —I tried everything to spare him. For his sake did I not strike up a friendship with that wretched fox Herod in the hope that he, as his sovereign, would be able to set him free? Did I not try to satisfy those Jewish hyenas by scourging their victim? Did I not give them a choice between their king and the murderer Barabbas, so as to force them to ask for the release of this Jesus? Till the end I declared that I found him innocent, and I washed my hands for all the world to see that his blood was not on me! Go to the Jews, then, who took it upon themselves —what do you want from me? Of what are you accusing me? Of what have you accused me all these years whenever you looked at me with your unbearable stare, with that look that destroyed our happiness . . ." He clenched his fists; was it anger? Was it fear? "What are you trying to tell me with that look?"

She took a step toward him and stretched out her arms. "That I have compassion on you, my beloved", she said, and nothing more. She put both arms around him and drew his head to her breast. I could see neither her face nor his; I perceived only the primordial tone of love, refined into that mercy which once in front of the courthouse in Jerusalem seemed to engulf the whole world. Nothing was left but the indestructible undestroyed bond between these two human beings: guilt and love had found one another.

For a while no one spoke. "My Claudia, my Claudia", his voice could scarcely be heard. Then, again after a while, he said more clearly: "What do you know about the people for whom you are pleading?"

Had her compassion won? But now from the street a vulgar noise arose that had been approaching for quite some time. We could hear the cry: "To the lions! Throw the Nazarenes to the lions! He who spares these criminals is no friend of Caesar!"

The Procurator started as though awaking from a dream —his face darkened.

Meanwhile the slave, who for a long while had been standing close by unnoticed, announced that the sedan chair was ready.

And now, noble Julia, I must once again admit to you with deep sorrow my own failure, which I already confessed to you in my first letter. I will never understand how I could have been so careless, for was it not the most logical thing in the world that Claudia, after interiorly finding her way back to her fellow believers, would also rejoin their community? Moreover, now she would feel the need to hurry to the Subura to warn those who were in danger; maybe she even thought that she, as the wife of the Procurator, could afford them some protection. Yes, certainly, all this was too obvious. And yet I did not notice the preparations she made in complete secrecy, for naturally she did not intend to draw me into a possible catastrophe, nor did she want me to interfere with her plan.

After the distressing conversation with her husband, she had retreated to her bedroom and expressly ordered me to leave her alone. So incomprehensibly unsuspecting was I that I did not notice her disappearance until evening, when I went to undress her for the night. I did not find her in the chamber, and yet it was strangely filled with her spirit—quite unexpectedly I had to think of that morning when she had awakened so overjoyed after the night of love early in her marriage. Today, though, evening was falling: the little statue of Eros that her husband had once given her stood forlorn in the room. Bewildered, as though a beloved person had just now departed forever, I remained standing at the threshold: Was not the charming god of love of my native land also the god of death, whom great Praxiteles depicted with a downturned torch in his hand? And already my eyes alit on the little three-legged bronze table beside the abandoned couch. The wax tablet that Claudia used each day to write down her notes for the household lay upon it. I read the lines: "I go to keep my husband from a second offense", I read. "Be consoled, my Praxedis, if I should not come back." Appalled, I dropped the tablet: From what place did she think she might not come back? It must be the Subura. Without delay I hastened there, but I arrived too late.

Rome lay in darkness as formerly Jerusalem had at the hour of the crucifixion. In the Subura, the garish laughter of the prostitutes was muted, and I encountered no one. Some deadly fear weighed upon the streets of the whole district. The house of the Nazarenes stood silent as a tomb in the middle of the night. The door had been battered down, and solitude yawned within. Trembling, I felt my way to the meeting room; its door, too, stood open: black, lonely night stared at me, yet from one corner of the room came the sound of desperate sobbing. Groping, I walked toward it—on the floor lay a dark figure; it was the Syrian woman. Shivering, I touched her shoulder—she recognized me in the dark by my voice.

"It is over," she stammered, "it is over! The Lord did not come, but the legionaries came instead—it is over—

it is over forever!'' She kept lamenting in this way. Only gradually did I manage to ask what had happened. Claudia, as I had suspected, had appeared in the assembly. The Syrian woman, in keeping with her childish confidence in the second coming of the Lord during the worst affliction of his followers, had hidden, so as to render the first honors to the One whom they awaited. Thus she herself had escaped arrest. From her hiding place, she had observed how Claudia stood in the way of the legionaries, who had arrived meanwhile, and demanded as the wife of Pontius Pilate that they set the captives free. She had been taunted and ridiculed and finally led off with the others—where? To prison? To their death? But the Syrian woman could give me no answer.

I hurried home, I sent messengers to the Procurator, who were to tell him about the arrest of my mistress and to beseech him to rescue her. But the Procurator was nowhere to be found. Meanwhile, sinister rumors made their way through the city: my mistress, they said, had been reported by one of her husband's slaves as a Nazarene. But the Procurator, too, had supposedly fallen into disfavor with the Emperor. I was in despair. Finally, I sent out my mistress' favorite slave, but the youth did not return at all. Several harrowing days passed in this way. At last a letter was brought to me by an unfamiliar Nazarene—it was in Claudia's handwriting. I broke the seal and read it:

Written in prison, a few hours before receiving the baptism of blood.

Greetings, blessings, and consolation to my beloved
Praxedis!

It was as God willed, and it will be as God wills: no
one can escape the mercy of Christ. God visited me again
in a dream as once before in Jerusalem. Once again I was
walking through centuries of temples and houses of prayer
—they had now become old and gray, just as a dying race
grows old and gray. In my heart was an abysmal sadness,
not because I knew that I had been sentenced to death,
but because I thought that I would have to die in vain.
For had not my whole life and love been one failure, repeated again and again? All these houses of God seemed
to me to be built on a deceptive foundation of faith—for
Christ's compassion could never be victorious on earth
—the earth being what it was, mercy could only shat-
ter against it. I ran from one temple to another trying
to reach the open air—there was no end of them, but
their architecture became increasingly bleak and empty, as
though now men could construct only outmoded forms
in which the soul no longer abided.

But suddenly this picture changed: I reached a room
that seemed even stranger than the ones before—the walls
made of an unknown material, the room wide open,
solemnly bare and flooded with light—on the altar nothing but the cross, the sign of death! A dense, fearful
crowd was huddled in this room, a choir sang the profession of faith: again the beloved name of my husband
resounded, but now it was no longer like a threatening
indictment, but rather as if the voices were clinging to
a final consolation in the sentence: Crucifixus etiam pro
nobis sub Pontio Pilato. At the same time I heard a distant
droning, as though tremendous storms were descending
upon the land and swiftly approaching—the walls of the
temple in which I found myself swayed. Once again the

choir started to sing with trembling voices: Crucifixus etiam pro nobis—my husband's name was swallowed up in the droning of a cosmic hymn—was this the end of the ages? My foot stopped short as though I dared not trespass. I felt the centuries coming apart like a brittle, rusted chain—the last temple wall fell, allowing a view of eternity—I saw coming in the clouds the same judgment seat that once had stood before the courthouse in Jerusalem, but on it sat, not my husband, but rather the One whom he had once condemned, and before him, in the place where the condemned man had stood, my husband was now standing, awaiting judgment. The One on the judgment seat, however, regarded him with the same look of mercy with which he had once looked at him in Jerusalem. At the same time I heard a voice: Be comforted, Claudia Procula, I am the Absolutely Other, whom you have always sought—I am the one who was victorious in defeat, I am the Origin and the Loneliness and the Triumph of Eternal Love—therefore, fear not: you will die the same death as I—you will die for the salvation of him who causes you to die.

Numb and shaken, I dropped the sheet—for the first time in my life, faith in Christ touched the depths of my soul.

At that moment, the door was flung open, and the Procurator burst in—was it really he? Was this tormented face twisted in scorn still the countenance of our self-assured master? A Roman citizen? Here any such dignity was hopelessly crushed—only a man who had been mastered by despair could look like this. He fell to his knees before my mistress' bed like a tree felled by the ax, he tore the wreath from his forehead, and he hammered on his chest with both fists. "I killed her, I killed her", he shouted unceasingly. I stood there numb with horror. Then I noticed that my mistress' favorite slave had followed him. His face, too, was ashen, even his lips.

"He saw our mistress die", he stammered. "The Emperor, that monster, betrayed him! He was sitting in the circus beside the Emperor, who gloated over his horror when she entered the arena with the other Nazarenes. They did not cry 'Morituri te salutant' [Those who are about to die salute you] as the gladiators do; they prayed the profession of their faith. I still hear her last words: 'Crucifixus etiam pro nobis sub Pontio Pilato . . .' "

At the mention of his name, the Procurator looked up. "Slave, give me that sword!" he groaned, and when the trembling youth hesitated: "Quickly, quickly, I cannot wait for death!" He seized the weapon from him.

But now I lay my hand on his, which was ready to thrust. With a strength that was not mine, I said, "Pontius Pilate, Claudia died as Christ died—because of you, but also for you . . ."

He looked at me out of his ruined countenance for a long time uncomprehendingly—suddenly his glance sank inward. He dropped the sword.

Do not ask me to say another word, noble Julia—my report is ended—I, too, had been persuaded by the look of the Crucified.

～

Plus Ultra

. . . But then, Reverend Mother, but then—I mean, when I again met His Majesty's eyes—then each time it was as though a movement in the depths of my soul emanated from that immovable gaze that was fixed on me, or, rather, a riot and a storm within me, and I could not tell whether its name was rapture or horror or both at once. No, as God is my witness, Reverend Mother, I could not have told its name until the day when Her Highness, the Lady Regent, drew me into that conversation that you ordered your obedient daughter to write down.

I saw the Lady Regent for the first time when Her Majesty's difficult pregnancy was drawing to a close. At that time, the Lady Regent appeared unexpectedly in Valladolid, right at the moment when the whole court was profoundly dismayed, for it was rumored that the doctors had not given a good prognosis for Her Majesty's confinement, which had just begun. Without further ado or announcement, the Lady Regent made her way at once to Her Majesty's chamber. From behind I saw her hurrying toward it: during the hasty journey, her widow's veil had shifted somewhat, so that her magnificent blond hair had billowed out beneath it; now the entire veil sank to her neck and set the tresses completely free: she veritably glowed in the dusky corridors of the castle, and as we followed her tall, slender figure, it seemed to us that a candle was being carried before us.

I saw the Lady Regent face to face for the first time on the following day, when Her Majesty's delivery was already over—with the appearance of the Lady Regent, she had unexpectedly taken a turn for the better. We— I mean the attendants of Her Majesty—were then introduced to the Lady Regent: her face beamed like that of a still youthful Empress-Mother in whose arms the heir to the throne had just been placed—and, indeed, so she was to be regarded by us, since His Majesty never called her anything but "Sa tante et très chère mère" [His aunt and dearest mother]. Even today the widow's veil could not completely shade the gold on her head. Everyone said that the Lady Regent looked just as radiant as after the triumphal imperial election of His Majesty, in which, as the whole world knew, her clever hands had played a major part. The Lady Regent said something gracious and cheerful to each of us ladies, but to me she spoke not a word; she only eyed me with a look, a look, Reverend Mother, that, although her eyes in no way resembled those of His Majesty in their shape and color, was so terribly similar to their expression that my knees began to give way beneath me—I thought I would no longer be able to rise from my profound curtsy.

On the evening of that same day, I was summoned by the Lady High Chamberlain. She had always maintained that I was much too young to serve at court, but the Empress retained me anyway because I was an orphan of noble lineage. Recently I had heard the Lady High Chamberlain say repeatedly that they would do well to send me back to the convent. Therefore, I was quite frightened when I was called to appear before her.

You know, Reverend Mother, that I was a quiet but unruly child; even when you were raising me, convent life filled me with repugnance, but now I thoroughly dreaded it. The Lady High Chamberlain looked at me coldly and sternly, but she said nothing about the convent; instead, she informed me that Her Majesty had released me from her service into that of the Lady Regent. That night I wept for many long hours; it seemed to me that I would die if I left this place.

I was not allowed to bid farewell to the Empress or to anyone at all. Although it was not stated, I was aware of it. No one seemed to notice my dismissal; no one seemed to want to notice it. The Lady High Chamberlain inconspicuously beckoned me aside and instructed me to be ready for Her Highness' departure. This did not take place as quietly and surprisingly as her arrival, but rather it was with great ceremony and in the presence of the whole court. His Majesty himself accompanied "sa tante et très chère mère" down the steps of the castle to the carriage. I walked, as I had been ordered, with the ladies of her retinue, who bowed elegantly and ceremoniously to every side. I bowed also, but no one wanted to notice it. It was as if I had become invisible. At the same time, though, it was as though I were made of glass; I thought everyone could see into my heart and knew also the reason for my dismissal. I myself did not know it, and I could not see into my heart—I assure you once again, Reverend Mother, by all that is holy: I could not! But I could see with my heart, with it I could almost see through myself, just as if I were made of glass. For although I did not once dare to raise my eyes to His Majesty, I suddenly became aware that his gaze was again fixed on me. The Lady Regent's carriage had now driven off; we could hear the wheels rolling away. His Majesty had turned around and was slowly climbing back up the stairs; on the top step I waited with another lady of Her Highness for the arrival of a second carriage. I saw His Majesty's slender, youthful figure, his pale, noble face with the slightly open mouth, as though it were always a bit thirsty, and the protruding lower lip of his line—I saw, saw once again that terrifying look, which welled up mightily from his imperial solitude and, as it were, rushed toward me, as though a living spring were bursting out of its stone vessel. This look took in my face, my figure, and all my members, indeed, my whole being and nature, in the way one can be encompassed by a man's look only once in a lifetime. I wanted to respond to this look—I, too, wanted with my own look to encompass His Majesty's face, figure, and whole being, as one can encompass a man only once in a lifetime. What am I saying: "I wanted"? It was as though I were being implored to give this response, in the final, very last hour. For, Reverend Mother, I had never given this response; the enormity of the delight and the horror that came over me at the sight of majesty had never allowed it. Nor did it allow it now. And yet I knew that the meaning of all the years of my life was compressed into these few seconds. But they were already over: after slowly climbing the stairs, the young ruler had reached the top, and now I walked down them with Her Highness' lady. Half fainting, I felt I was being lifted into the

carriage. And now the whole world sank, all the magnif-
icence of my youth and all the hope of my future life—
to me it was as if I had died and been banished to eternal
damnation.

No one had bid me farewell at the court in Valladolid,
and no one greeted me at the court in Malines, either.
It seemed that everyone had made an agreement that I
had always been there. The Lady Regent accepted the little services I performed for her like something to which
she had long been accustomed. The ladies of her court
treated me familiarly, as if they were trying to make me
believe I had only dreamed about Valladolid. I pretended
to be as they wanted—being a proper little court lady, I
knew how to do that, or rather I thought I knew, just as
I knew how to make my profound, ceremonious curtsies. Indeed, in the retinue of an empress, one becomes
proficient in the stern art of courtly obedience! Ah, but
how much wordless rebellion can be hidden beneath the
deepest curtsy, how stormily a heart can beat under a
satin-smooth court gown! Not until I took that gown off
in the evening and lay down to sleep did I let the mask
fall. I yearned for that moment all day long.

The attendants of the Lady Regent did not sleep in
the so-called Regency, where she herself lived with her
counselors, but rather in the old palace of the Duke of
Burgundy located across from it. Our chambers were
crowded together like cells in a cloister. This caused me
some anxiety at first, but the old ducal palace had thick
walls, and the sound of sobbing could not travel from
one room to the next.

Darkness lay upon the street beneath my window, for in Malines the night was not blue and crystal clear as in Valladolid but, rather, velvet-black; one could see no end to the gloom. The air that came in was damp and cool; my feet were often chilly, so that for a long time I could not fall asleep. Again and again, I heard the hours strike in the stout old tower of Saint Rumbold's Cathedral. Moreover, I often fell asleep without praying, but this did not happen to me because I wanted to turn away from God; rather, it was as though suddenly there was no room left for God in my heart—now there was room in it only for my yearning for Valladolid. When I got up in the morning, the linens of my bed were completely soaked with tears—often I had wept through the entire night. These tears were more profoundly refreshing than sleep, but I wept in my sleep, too.

I always had to get up before the dew and the dawn in order to cool my eyes, so that no one could tell I had spent the night in tears. This took me a long time, for the fountain of my eyes did not want to stop flowing—often I could no longer tell what was water and was tears.

The Lady Regent was a kind and considerate mistress to her entire court, except that she could not tolerate little flirtations; her young attendants had to be very wary of those. Only great love, they used to say, met with her protection and her special delight. Neither of these things concerned me, I thought. Meanwhile, the Lady Regent proved to be a kind mistress to me as well, but I was unable to show her any gratitude whatsoever for it. Reverend Mother, I must confess to you: the only feeling that still found room within me besides my yearning for Valladolid was resentment toward the Lady Regent, for I still thought she was the one at whose request I had been dismissed from the service of the Empress, although I could not imagine why she wanted me at her side. Often this resentment welled up in me so furiously that I was tempted to do her some harm. She possessed a ruby-glass goblet, which she had received as a present from her imperial nephew after he had been elected the Holy Roman Emperor. In the evening, when I had to hand her the sleeping potion that the doctors had prescribed for her on account of her bad nights, sometimes the desire to drop it came over me, for I knew it was particularly precious to her. Or else I felt the need to kick her white whippet when she had commanded me to take it downstairs into the garden and to bring it back again. It would have happened, too, had the little animal not known how to protect itself. Its head was as fine and delicate as though it had been carved out of ivory, and its understanding, too, was just as fine: it noticed everything and was also allowed to be present at everything, even when the Lady Regent conferred with the estates of the realm. Then it would lie at her feet, apparently asleep, but as soon as one of the lords made a move to defy her, it instantly growled. And even when my resentment against the Lady Regent sprang up within me, it was immediately aware of it. Then suddenly it would raise its narrow head, strangely alert, and look at me, but it would not growl. But then the Lady Regent would raise her head, too, and look at me: and then, Reverend Mother, then every time all my resentment instantly faded, died, and scattered as though in a shiver of joy, for again it truly seemed to me that His Majesty's eyes were looking at me. Afterward I had to keep asking myself: Of whom is the Lady Regent so fond? Whom does she love so much? After all, one looks at another person that way only if one is inexpressibly fond of somebody! But even though I asked this question, nevertheless, Reverend Mother, I still did not know what had happened to me. My confessor later maintained that I should have known, but what does a monk know about the heart of a maiden? With God as my witness, I knew nothing about mine, unless there is a knowledge of what one does not know.

In the morning, when I glided down the stairs in the old ducal palace to report for my duties across the way in the Regency, I always had to go past several apartments where (the ladies had told me) His Majesty and his little sisters the duchesses had lived as children, when the Lady Regent was still acting as a foster mother to them. They said that she still kept there the children's playthings with which the little princely personages had once amused themselves. I would have been all too glad to enter those rooms sometime; indeed, my yearning to do so was almost as great as my yearning for Valladolid —I had the notion that if I could just once see and touch those toys, I would become less heavy-hearted. I always used to linger, too, when I had to walk by those rooms, and sometimes it seemed to me as though I heard a noise from within like the whining of a little doll who is being hugged or like notes struck on the clavichord that I knew had once been obtained for His Majesty. In short, it appeared to me that the old playthings in those rooms had somehow started to move. If there had not been so many lords and ladies walking through the corridor, I could not have resisted the temptation to go inside.

Finally, one day—the corridor was completely empty and deserted for the first time—I opened the door. There I saw a little girl standing upright in her crib and holding a big doll on her arm. She looked as terribly familiar to me as the childhood portraits of the little duchesses, but at the same time terribly mysterious as well, as if a royal child were being kept hidden there—and the royal children had long since outgrown the room! I stood there so startled and bewildered that I could scarcely keep my composure. "Who are you?" I managed to stammer.

"And who are you?" the child asked haughtily in reply. It sounded as if she were saying: How dare you address me at all? Meanwhile, from the other side, a fat old attendant came in, saw my astonishment, and told me in a tone of voice swelling with pride: "This is the little daughter of the beautiful Johanna van der Gheenst—we have been sick for a long time, but tomorrow we will get up again for the first time." . . .

Everything at this court in Malines left me quite indifferent, but I would all too gladly have learned who Johanna van der Gheenst was. I often listened to see whether this name would ever be mentioned in the conversation of Her Highness' attendants, but no one ever spoke it—they were just as silent about it as they had been about my own arrival from Valladolid. And I was too proud to ask, although I could not have said why exactly the question about Johanna van der Gheenst injured my pride, but the fact was that it did. I have already said, Reverend Mother, that there is a kind of knowledge of what one does not know.

The attendants of the Lady Regent did not sit down as often at their embroidery frames as the ladies of Her Majesty in Valladolid. The Lady Regent needed us for other business. Her antechambers were crowded with messengers from foreign courts and representatives of the estates of the realm, its ostentatious clergy, its defiant nobility, and its wealthy tradesmen, not to mention its wise, cautious councilors. After all, the Lady Regent governed this land for His Majesty, and everything that otherwise would come to a ruler came here to a Lady Governor. So her ladies always had to be prepared to welcome those who arrived, to entertain with wit and lute playing those who were waiting, and sometimes even to put off or send away the unwelcome with a skillful speech. Her Highness' attendants also held their little heads much higher than the ladies at Valladolid, as though they imagined that they themselves knew something about ruling. They also spoke about many things that never concerned the ladies of the Empress. I heard there for the first time about the predicament that the terrible sack of the city of Rome caused for His Majesty's reign, about the Holy Father's anger at him, that the menacing Turk was at the borders of Hungary, and that nevertheless peace with His Majesty the King of France was just not forthcoming. For, as the Lady Regent's attendants used to say, men nowadays knew only how to wage wars, but they could no longer make peace. And as they spoke, they would put their little heads together, as though they meant to set up a tent over the endangered world with their lace veils.

When foreign couriers rode into the courtyard of the Regency, my heart always leapt into my throat, and I sought an excuse to stand at the window and look out to see whether it might be an imperial courier from Valladolid. Yes, Reverend Mother, I was so childish that it seemed to me that I could be happy for a moment if only I caught sight of the insignia of an imperial courier. Once, when I really did see the longed-for sign, I ran down the stairs of the Regency and into the courtyard with my train held high and rushed like an impetuous lad over to the rider's horse, so that its foam flew into my hair, while Her Highness' whippet, which had run after me, yelped joyfully all around me. "Sir, give me the letter, so that I may take it to Her Highness!" I cried. But he did not give it to me, and I had to climb the stairs again in shame.

The Countess Croy stood at the top and was about to scold me roundly because I had taken my train under my arm. But then the Lady Regent stepped out of the door and said, "Dear Countess, who won just now in this race —my whippet or our little Arabella? I watched their competition from the window; help me decide!" At that the Countess Croy could say nothing more against me; she turned red in her old gray face like a young maiden; I myself, however, must have gone deathly pale, for now the Lady Regent eyed me once again with that look— with that look—Reverend Mother, alas, I have already spoken about it.

The Lady Countess Croy was the first lady at the court of the Regent. She had already served her mother, when the latter had still been the young unmarried daughter of the Duke of Burgundy, and they said that as a child the Lady Regent had sat on her lap. It often happened, too, that she still addressed her as Lady Archduchess, but the Lady Regent did not mind hearing that, because this title reminded her that she was the daughter of an emperor.

Because the Countess Croy loved the Lady Regent exceedingly, she could not abide me. For although I myself always supposed that I was as proficient in the stern art of silence and dissimulation as in my profound, ceremonious curtsies, she still knew very well that I had an aversion to the Lady Regent and in my heart was constantly rebelling against her—indeed, only in my own eyes was I a proper little court lady; in reality, I was a wild, desperate child, and everything that went on within me was plain to see. And the Lady Countess Croy had sharp eyes that got to the bottom of all violations of etiquette and all the hidden recesses of hearts. Surely she also knew about the nights I had spent weeping—I could have sworn that she slept with her eyes open like an old hare. She continually pointed out to me that the Lady Regent was much too lenient with me, and the Lady Regent certainly was that. She did not often speak with me, but she always protected me when the Countess Croy tried to scold me. But I held this against her, like everything else, for I always thought she knew very well she had to make amends to me for something. Indeed, I was so resentful of the Lady Regent that I was unwilling to see any good in her at all. When others praised her, I remained silent, and the Lady Regent was praised a great deal. I often heard people say that she could rule like a man, but once I also heard a great lord

of the land object, "No, she does not rule like a man
—her father, Emperor Max, tried to rule us like a man,
and we resisted him. She rules like a woman, and thereby
she has vanquished us. For it does the defiant estates of
this country good to listen to a woman. A man alone
makes for a lot of turbulence, but where a woman has a
hand in things, the world is restored to balance." Thereupon a third voice said: "Yes, Her Highness' secret is that
she rules like a man and a woman in one person—you
might believe that she still has her husband with her."
This statement astonished me, because I thought that the
Lady Regent had long since forgotten her husband. Ad-
mittedly, she never put off her widow's veil, but the revealing blond strands of her hair always protruded somewhere, as though to proclaim that the Lady Regent was
not a real widow. Moreover, she was always brightly and
gaily dressed and liked to see bright, gay clothing around
her; even the walls of her workroom had to be so clad.
Jovial green forest trees were woven into the tapestries
that hung there, so that upon entering you thought you
could hear birds singing. No, I almost could not believe
that the Lady Regent was a widow, and I thought I knew
all about widows: ever since His Majesty had waged the
great, terrible wars in Italy and France, there were many
lonely women in Spain. And then in that country there
was also Queen Juana, who had once gone mad beside
her husband's corpse. You yourself, Reverend Mother,
told me how she fled cross-country with her husband's
coffin, so as not to have to allow her subjects to lower it
into the grave; that again and again she had them open this
coffin so that she could kiss the dead man on the mouth.

You said then that this behavior of Queen Juana was horrible, Reverend Mother, but I was pleased by it. Yes, I thought that a proper widow would have to love death —the Lady Regent, however, loved life: she loved the cheerful, industrious people she ruled for His Majesty; she loved their wealth and their defiance, their self-willed nobility and their ostentatious tradesmen. She loved her own light, festive garments and the jovial forest trees in the tapestries on her walls; she loved her clever little dog; she still loved the toys of the royal children whom she had once raised; she loved them and above all her imperial nephew; she loved his crown; and then she also loved —this was my final discovery—that mysterious little girl whom I had encountered some time before in the former apartment of the royal children.

The girl was well again, and I saw her every day when her old nurse took her to walk in the garden. Furthermore, the girl sometimes came over from the old ducal palace to the Regency. On her light little feet, she would run unabashedly through the brightly mirrored halls to the workroom of the Lady Regent, who used to expect her at a particular time. If she was not yet ready, the mysterious child, who was not at all shy, would knock on her door. Her Highness' ladies would place their fingers on their lips and whisper, "Quiet, quiet, Her Highness is having an audience!" But the old nurse, who followed the child, would say insolently, "We take no orders here, for we are the daughter of the beautiful Johanna van der Gheenst, and someday, when we are grown up, we too will be a Duchess."

The mysterious little girl had immediately recognized

me as the one who had once barged into her room. Every time she saw me, she stopped, as though rooted to the ground, and proudly sized me up from top to bottom with her big, childish eyes, as though she wanted to ask me again: And who are you? But then, before I could give an answer, she suddenly spun around like a top on her little tapered heel and ran away posthaste. I, however, veritably ran in the other direction—it was as if we had scared each other to death.

And if the mysterious little girl was with the Lady Regent, the latter took her onto her lap and tenderly caressed her. If I was on duty then and was standing nearby, every time the thought ran through my mind: in precisely this way the Lady Regent caressed the little duchesses, too, and in just this way she caressed the boyish head of her imperial nephew—yes, just like that and with the same hands! And now all at once I felt nothing but a desire to kiss the Lady Regent's hands quickly and inconspicuously. This desire was so strong that the whippet at her feet sensed it once again, but the Regent sensed it, too— she smiled at me, as though she understood everything that was going on within me, indeed, as though she, of all people, was the only human being who understood me, even though I did not understand myself. And at that, all my resentment toward her collapsed once again like a house of cards—I no longer knew whether I loved or hated her; I only knew that she herself loved me.

Yes, the Lady Regent loved many things and many people, but she most certainly did not love her husband— that was settled, as far as I was concerned. But when I once childishly and unthinkingly ventured to say so to Mademoiselle von Bentink—she was the attendant of Her Highness who was closest to me in age—my interlocutor looked at me wide-eyed with astonishment and said, "Arabella, have you never heard of the name Brou?" Of course I had often heard it mentioned, for not only envoys from the courts and the estates came to call on the Lady Regent, but also great artists from all over the world, architects, sculptors, and painters, and of all her guests these were her favorites. With them she conferred for hours on end on account of a beautiful church she was having built in distant Savoy, her former duchy. Her attendants said that this church was a peerless gem; one might think that it was not built of stones at all but, rather, had blossomed from sheer tenderness and love, like the calyx of a mystical rose or like the affectionate heart of a woman—and from such a heart this church, too, had sprung up. "All beautiful churches", the ladies used to say, "are built by men, but this one is designed by a woman, and the builders have only executed Her Highness' ideas. And therefore this church will never be finished, for the yearning of which it was born is never-ending."

When the Countess Croy heard this sort of talk, her old gray face again turned red like that of a young maiden. "This church most assuredly will be finished", she said vehemently. "You God-forsaken maids, do you mean to parrot the same slander as the clerics in Rome? As if the Lady Regent were not sufficiently pious!"

For a long time, though, I had noticed that the Lady Regent was not very pious; of course, I was constantly on the lookout for her faults, and although I myself was not at all pious, in her case it seemed to me to be a fault, and I was glad about it. Granted, she conscientiously performed all her religious duties, for one can indeed do that, Reverend Mother, without being pious—oh, one most assuredly can do that! It is, after all, so easy to go to church, kneel down, and read the prescribed prayers, but to lift up one's heart to heaven, when so many threads tie it down to earth, that is difficult!

We went to Mass each day with the Lady Regent, a dignified, devout train. She herself would then carry in her hands her father's prayer book, the renowned volume beautifully illuminated by Master Dürer. Her attendants followed her, heads bowed like hers, their little trains charmingly arranged behind them, their rosaries delicately wrapped around their fingers like jeweled chains, and I myself was among them, surely an edifying sight like all the others, and yet I was so far removed from God— alas, immeasurably far, much farther even than the distance from Valladolid to Malines . . .

Just as I had noticed that the Lady Regent was not pious, so too I had noticed that some secret or other hovered around that church in Brou. Once a great French lord, who was staying at the time in Malines as an envoy, asked: "What does His Majesty actually say about the construction of this church?" The ladies of Her Highness smiled and evaded the question: "No one knows, Monsieur." The Countess Croy, however, cut them short: "We most assuredly do know, dear children! His Majesty always agrees with his *très chère tante et mère*." The French lord was quite obviously delighted with that, but I thought he was no longer thinking about the church in Brou but, rather, thought we were hinting that the terms of peace between his ruler and our Imperial Majesty ought to be entrusted to the Lady Regent—for this conversation took place shortly before Her Highness traveled to Cambrai.

At that time couriers from Valladolid arrived almost daily in Malines, but I no longer ran down to them in the courtyard; rather, I sought an excuse to busy myself in the Lady Regent's workroom, if only with her little whippet's silky fur coat. Whereupon the Lady Regent seemed never to notice me, although the Countess Croy eagerly made signs that I should be sent away before she read a letter to Her Highness. The Countess Croy was obliged to do this frequently, because the beautiful, warm eyes of Her Highness had been ailing for some time, and if she wanted to read, she had to make use of someone else's eyes. Then I would fight a spirited battle between my resentment toward her and my yearning for the letters, because I knew that my ability to stay depended on the Lady Regent. On the other hand, I did not know what I actually expected to gain from listening to these letters, for of course all of them just came from dusty chanceries, yet they spoke about His Majesty. Every time his name was mentioned, it seemed to me that lightning struck beside me; I was frightened to death, and yet I continued to listen longingly for it. The Countess Croy was always somewhat excited when she read aloud the letters from the imperial chancery, for she lived in constant fear that they might announce the outbreak of a new war, even though they spoke again and again about making peace. But even the Lady Regent was sometimes uneasy;

these letters obviously did not please her, and although the Countess Croy had said to the French lord that His Majesty always agreed with her, now he seemed to be not at all of the same mind with her. Once, while the Countess Croy was reading aloud to her, one of her councilors was announced. The Lady Countess immediately stood up and went out. I knew I should do the same, for the councilors always wanted to confer with Her Highness alone. But I buried my face in the whippet's coat and pretended to be blind and deaf; but Her Highness remained silent about my presence—it was as though she knew what spell kept me there. I ought to have thanked her for this with all my heart and with my eyes, but being dependent on her goodness filled me with indignation, and yet I *was* dependent on her—she could have sent me away like the Countess Croy. Why did she not actually do so? It was as if she approved of my yearning. Meanwhile, the Lady Regent's councilor had entered. She called to him: "Just think, Monsieur Des Barres, His Majesty still insists on the harsh terms of peace from Madrid; he will not drop the paragraph dealing with Bourgogne."

Monsieur Des Barres replied cautiously: "As victor, His Majesty of course has the right to humiliate France."

The Lady Regent pushed her chair back a bit, as sometimes happened when the defiant estates of the land tried to rebel against her—I say "tried" because she could handle them—and this was, I must admit, often wonderful to behold.

"What do you mean, humiliate France?" she asked.

"Can the humiliation of France perhaps be His Majesty's aim? Ah, I do not ever want to see a prince as a victor—victory makes one narrow-minded!"

Monsieur Des Barres bowed. "Honor to Your Highness", he said. "Glory be to the clemency of a kindly woman's heart."

But the Lady Regent cut him short: "No, Monsieur Des Barres, you misunderstand me. The point here is not to praise a clement woman's heart; the point is to recognize that clemency and fairness are part of common sense. The Turk is drawing near to the gates of Hungary and is threatening Christendom—this is not about France, Monsieur Des Barres, it is about the West! His Majesty needs his hands free in order to ward off the Turks, but His Majesty apparently does not want his hands free."

Now Monsieur Des Barres suddenly became serious. "Does this mean that Her Highness will not go to Cambrai?" he asked.

The Lady Regent stood up: "No, it means that I must go to Cambrai." And after that, with unusual warmth: "My God, I held His Majesty as a child on my lap, after all—he was a self-willed, taciturn child, but he was also a magnanimous child—even as a little boy, he had a sense of dignity! When I used to take his little head in my hands and teach him the words of salutation that were supposed to please his imperial grandfather, he accurately repeated after me even the things that went against the grain—I want to take his head into my hands again."

A quiet time came now for the old ducal palace. The Lady Regent was in Cambrai, and together with the Queen

Mother of France, she concluded peace for the two rulers who could not bring about peace. Meanwhile, the clever ladies of Her Highness had to content themselves for a while with sitting down at their embroidery frames like the ladies in Valladolid. The Lady Regent had left behind a tapestry, intended as a gift for the Knights of the Golden Fleece. Prominently displayed in the middle was the coat of arms of the archducal house, to the right and the left the mottos of His Majesty and Her Highness. The motto of Her Highness read: "Fortune, Infortune—font une", "Fortune, misfortune—much the same", but His Majesty's motto was "Nondum". The uncivil ladies of Her Highness often made fun of it: "Nondum", they used to say, "means 'Not yet.' With a motto like that, His Majesty truly could not bring about a conclusion of peace!" This mockery of the ill-bred ladies offended me very much, for I knew from the Spanish tournaments that the "Nondum" of His Majesty did not mean "There is still time for that" but, rather, meant "Not enough has been accomplished yet." It was not a word of hesitation but, rather, the exalted, throbbing word referring to an objective that is all too high. Once, when the ladies were again making their familiar sarcastic gibes, I jumped up like a little lion and told them that they misunderstood the motto. Now they nudged each other, giggling, but the Countess Croy rushed over to me and said that I should be quiet and see to my work, namely, the motto of Her Highness, which I had been told to embroider. But I could not understand that motto at all, and I made one mistake after another in my work, so that I had to rip out my stitches over and over again. Since the Countess

Croy was becoming impatient, she wrote out the saying for me and laid the slip of paper beside me.

We were still not quite done with our tapestry when the Lady Regent returned. She really had brought about peace, not the evil peace of Madrid, but her peace, the famous "Ladies' Peace of Cambrai". It seemed as if the Countess Croy was right after all and His Majesty at last was in agreement with his *très chère tante et mère*.

The Lady Regent appeared one day to inspect our work. I heard her talking with the Countess Croy about His Majesty's motto and pricked up my ears as I used to for the hoofbeats of the imperial couriers. In doing so, however, I bent even lower over my work, but now the Lady Regent was going from one attendant to the next, and I thought: if only she would pass me by! Suddenly I felt the wet snout of her whippet on my hand. The Lady Regent was standing beside me, and she had already caught sight of the Countess Croy's slip of paper.

"Do you like my motto so much, Arabella, that you wrote it down for yourself?" she asked.

I replied defiantly, "Your Highness, someone wrote it down for me, because I was making too many mistakes in my embroidery. I do not understand the motto."

She said, "Now try and see whether you have more success with His Majesty's motto; it no longer reads 'Nondum', though, but rather 'Plus ultra'. His Majesty changed it recently because it could be misunderstood, but I hear that you understood it." Then she instructed the Countess that she should employ me from henceforth on this motto. I would have liked most to throw my arms around the Lady Regent at that moment, and yet in no way did I understand what she wanted to tell me thereby; no, Reverend Mother, no, I only understood that after a long time had passed.

Since the Lady Regent's return from Cambrai, her ladies held their little heads much higher than before. "Yes, so it had to come about," they said, "so it had to come about! In Cambrai Her Highness helped a king and an emperor out of their impasse—now she will have to take on the Holy Father as well"—for between the latter and His Majesty there was still no peace. And at that time in Malines they really were expecting a high-ranking prelate from Rome who, as they believed, was supposed to make every effort with the Lady Regent to mediate between His Holiness and His Majesty. The ladies were triumphant; only the Countess Croy seemed a little subdued, as though the high-ranking guest filled her with apprehension.

It so happened that on the day of the audience of this prelate, I was supposed to be on duty in the Lady Regent's antechamber. Before I entered it, the Countess Croy told me that I might keep on hand the plans for the church in Brou—why, I did not know, for the prelate, after all, was coming on account of the peace treaty.

Now when I took the portfolio from its locked drawer, I happened to drop it out of clumsiness. As it fell, the flap opened, and the papers fluttered to the floor, so that I had to pick them up, and, in so doing, I saw them for the first time. There was the exterior ground plan, drawn exactly and without ornamentation as the builders required it. There was also the ground plan for the interior, just as strict and bare in its lines, as such plans are wont to be. There were also patterns for the stonemasons, pertaining to all sorts of ornamentation and decoration; indeed, there were a large number of these on hand. These sheets, too, were designed for the hand that sculpts and not for the eye that enjoys. But then one sheet stood out that was beautifully water-colored with gentle and yet forceful tones, meant no longer for the sculptor's hand but, rather, for the eye of the beholder. On this sheet, the church was completed, and the viewer saw into its interior and, yes, understood why the Regent's ladies called this church a mystical rose: I would not have been surprised if someone had told me that it had the fragrance of flowers as other churches smell of incense. And it really was, too, as if a woman's hand had erected it, such a tender love was revealed inside: this love seemed to have devised and shaped every ornament and every decoration, every figure therein; it filled up the whole space so perfectly that at first I did not notice what was missing in it. In the choir, namely, where ordinarily in a church the high altar rises, rose a richly decorated monument like a tabernacle. On the sarcophagus lay, depicted in stone, a sleeping man of great noble beauty. Around him crowded a host of little guardian angels, who had taken his weapons from him so that he could stretch out more comfortably. He lay there quite defenseless, as though he had sunk into the arms of that great, gentle but strong love that surrounded him on all sides—the whole sublime space of the church seemed to be there only for this slumbering figure, every ornament therein and every decoration designed and appointed for him alone, as though a tender heart again and again had devised new glories to bestow on him. Suddenly I could think of nothing but: Oh, how the Lady Regent loved this man, how she loves him still! Oh, who could love as she does?!

But now the Lady Regent's call resounded from the adjoining room, and I went in to bring her the requested portfolio. She sat in her high armchair, and behind the back of it loomed the splendid forest trees of her wall tapestry, and as always some of her blond hair protruded beneath her widow's veil, so that it was as though little lights were dancing about her face and she were sitting in the warm sun. The prelate was plainly not sitting in the sun, but, rather, winter snow appeared to lie around his still-young head, in whose countenance pomp and asceticism made an odd rendezvous. As I proffered to my mistress the item she had requested, he bowed toward her, while his hand, anticipating hers, took the portfolio with a lordly gesture that was scarcely concealed. Simultaneously the whippet at the Regent's feet awoke with a start and growled. The Lady Regent blushed and suppressed an indulgent smile.

I made my curtsy and withdrew again into the antechamber. Behind me it became alarmingly still. For a while I heard only the rustling of the papers, which the prelate turned over slowly.—You should know, Reverend Mother, that the lobby was closed off from the audience chamber only by a tapestry, so that every sound from inside could be heard easily.

Finally the cool voice of the clerical lord said: "Madame, a year and a day ago I already had the honor and privilege of reminding Your Highness that His Episcopal Grace longingly awaits the opportunity to consecrate the church in Brou and to dedicate it to its spiritual purpose, but I still miss the high altar that Your Highness surely ordered long ago."

The Lady Regent hesitated momentarily, as though she were considering a careful evasion of the question as her answer. Finally, though, she said frankly: "I have given no orders for the high altar, Monseigneur."

The prelate, too, hesitated for a few seconds, then said just as frankly: "So they were right after all to start legal proceedings against Your Highness before our tribunal in Rome—this church is not to the honor of God; it was, as the whole world already maintains, really built to honor your beloved husband. Madame, this church is a great heathen, and I fear that its builder is one, too."

"And if I were a heathen, Monseigneur," the Regent replied with fine irony, "I do not say that I am one— could the Rome of the Borgia popes and of Leo the Tenth turn that into a reproach against me?"

Now the cool voice of the prelate was colored with restrained emotion: "Your Highness is mistaken, we are no longer the opulent Rome of the Borgia popes and of Leo the Tenth. His Majesty's hordes of mercenaries made sure that we would have to take a terrible penance upon ourselves. With the *Sacco di Roma* a new generation has grown up among us, and this generation has done penance as never before. Truly the body of the Eternal City has no member that has not made atonement—we priests have gone gray as a result. But his Imperial Majesty will have to make atonement as well; one does not sin with impunity against a holy place."

The Lady Regent's chair moved as it often did in the presence of the defiant estates. "No one", she said rapidly, "can regret more profoundly than His Majesty the fact that his victory was paid for by the plundering of the Eternal City. His Majesty did not intend that atrocity."

Now I thought I could tell from the prelate's voice that a triumphant smile flitted over his features. "Your Highness speaks of an imperial victory", he said. "I am sorry to find you for the second time in error. At Rome, his Imperial Majesty was not victorious as at Pavia but, rather, was decisively defeated by his own army—with the Sack of Rome, His Majesty forfeited the victory. A beaten, captured king of France is a beaten, captured king, but a beaten, captured pope immediately becomes a glorious and mighty pope: all Christendom will fall at the feet of such a pope, as though Christ himself had been insulted in him." Then, emphatically: "His Holiness has sent to Valladolid his conditions for the absolution of His Majesty; they are of no concern to us here. Let us return then to the church in Brou . . ."

The Regent interrupted him: "Are you speaking to me on behalf of Rome?"

"Not yet," the prelate replied meaningfully, "but it could be that very soon I may have to speak to Your Highness on behalf of Rome. However, I am still speaking as a friend and warning you as an adviser."—The rest escaped me. Finally I caught these words: "Madame, I recommend that you offer up to God your sorrow as a widow, bid farewell to the desires of earthly life, and turn your attention to heavenly aspirations—a proper widow ought to die to the world."

Again the Lady Regent's chair moved, and immediately afterward I hear her gentle, kindly laughter. "Yes", she said—it sounded like a jest—"that is just what I expect from you priests! No sooner have you escaped the blatant sensuality of the Borgia era than you start again now with your contempt of the world. In your view, everything was put here only in order to be overcome and offered up to heaven. But someone who is supposed to shape and rule the world must not despise it; rather, he must be able to love this world and embrace it."

"Well," said the prelate calmly, "let us dismiss the question about contempt of the world. But what about the question of God? Your Highness is building for a mortal something that befits the Eternal alone—you hesitate to set up the altar to your Creator—you refuse to acknowledge God; that is the terrible secret of Brou that Rome cannot endure."

Once again a silence ensued; then the Lady Regent said softly and proudly: "I do not refuse to acknowledge God, Monseigneur, how could a human being presume to do that? But there is no room for God in my heart. Perhaps the room in this heart is too narrow, perhaps someday grace will expand it—for now it embraces nothing as it does my beloved husband: because he was a man, I love mankind; because he was a prince, I am willing to be a princess; because for me he is not dead, I can live. For me the church in Brou is not a tomb but, rather, the place where death was vanquished, because for love there is no separation, Monseigneur; love compensates for any separation. In Brou I can still prepare my husband's resting place; there I can lavish my tenderness on him; there I offer him again and again everything he loved about me and seek for myself the willingness and strength to live. For again, someone who is supposed to shape and rule the world must also be able to embrace it, and I embrace it in my beloved husband."

There was something compelling and enthralling in her speech, something that in its exuberance was thrilling, a devotion and a sweet strength that swept me away, like Queen Juana when she threw herself onto her husband's coffin, except that the Lady Regent wanted to shower death, not with kisses, as she had done, but rather with life. I perceived very well the terrifying element in her words, yet I did not shrink back from it; rather, my heart greeted it and rejoiced. I still heard the cool voice of the prelate, but only from a great distance: "Madame, I thank you for the honesty of your declaration—I believe I understand you completely now. Your Highness should leave your state as a widow and enter once more into the married state. Your Highness misses the joys of marriage, and unfortunately you have not hitherto been blessed with children. If Your Highness could decide to choose another husband, the question of Brou would resolve itself."

Now the Lady Regent stood up quickly, youthfully, almost stormily. I heard the rustling of her brocade dress. "Monseigneur," she said agitatedly, "I regret every word that I spoke to you! Love does not mean the choice of a state in life or sensual pleasure. Nor does love love on account of the blessing of children. Rather, love breaks in like a ray of light from another world so as to brighten ours, and I wish to entrust myself to this ray on my earthly journey. God will not condemn me on account of love, and now let us end this conversation." Immediately thereafter the prelate left the room.

I was still as though inebriated and stunned by what I had heard, and so it did not occur to me to kneel down for his blessing, which he carelessly bestowed as he went past. Reverend Mother, how am I supposed to describe to you my condition? The Lady Regent's words stormed and exulted within me. Now my thought was no longer as before: Oh, who could ever love as she does?! Because I could do it, I really could! It was as if all the doors within me suddenly flew open like the gilded side panels of a shrine, and I looked down for the first time into my own heart. Unintentionally I stretched out my arms —it was as though I were embracing the image therein: O Reverend Mother, I was so blissfully happy! Finally I knew what had happened to me, finally I knew that I loved and whom I loved!

Suddenly the warm, deep voice of the Lady Regent said beside me: "Arabella, did you hear my discussion with the prelate?"

I was trembling so much that I had to hold on to the tabletop in front of me, and it, too, trembled when I touched it, so that the bowl that stood on it began to clatter. "O Madame," I whispered, "Madame, you know that I was not allowed to leave my post."

She replied: "I know that, Arabella." As she said this, she took my head between her hands, tilted it back a bit, and then said once again: "I know it—I know it all." Oh, that look, Reverend Mother, that look—now finally I understood its mystery, too! That is how one looked when one had fallen incurably in love, and that—that is how the Emperor had looked at me! Not only did I love, I was loved as well! Once again I was overawed with incomparable bliss; it was almost a swoon that robbed me of all my strength, but also of any ability to grasp the unheard-of, indeed, presumptuous nature of this love— all that I could grasp now was the love itself. Everything else was as if destroyed, trampled underfoot, and scattered like dust—I thought I was dying. The bowl on the table to which I was clinging rattled so much it could have shattered—had the Lady Regent not put her arm around me, I would have slumped to the ground.

She held me quietly for a while in her embrace. Then she said: "Arabella, I brought you here like a little sleeping child, and you were angry with me, because you understood neither yourself nor me. But now you have awakened, and I can speak with you. They wanted to send you to the convent, and there you would have been ruined, for there you would have had to die to your love; but I loved your love, I wanted it to live, and it can live, for love knows no separation. You just heard that. You must not desire anything, but you may love, and that is enough. Do you now understand why I took you with me?"

But I did not understand her, no, Reverend Mother, now I no longer understood her! How could she compare herself with me?! She had lowered into the grave a husband whose love she had enjoyed, but I was supposed to bury in my heart someone I had never embraced? She had tasted every happiness and every delight, while I had only the bliss of yearning and longing; she was still allowed to show tenderness to a dead man, and I had not even returned the loving glance of a living man—I began to weep with heartbreaking sobs.

She hugged me maternally. "Poor child," she said, "poor child! Can I do nothing else for you but to commend you to the strength of your own love?"

"Madame, how can you ask such a thing? Surely you know what you can do for me", I exclaimed. "Oh, send me back to Valladolid, send me back! Allow me just one day there, just one single day—I beg you on my knees!" While I spoke, it seemed to me that my own heart was enveloping me in flames and that I would burn up if I were not allowed to go away. "Send me back! Send me back!" I cried incessantly. She looked at me sadly, and finally she said: "It would not help you at all, Arabella, if I granted your wish. Who do you think it was who wanted to send you to the convent?"

I said without hesitation, "It was Her Majesty, the Empress."

She replied, "No, it was the Emperor."

How was I to understand that? After all, I was loved! She guessed my thought: "Precisely because you were loved", she said.

Questions raced through my head: Was it for my sake? Was it to spare me, was it to protect me? Alas, Reverend Mother, a maiden who loves always thinks that her beloved can act toward her only out of love!

Now the Lady Regent shook her head reluctantly: "No, little fool," she said, "it was not for your sake, it was for the sake of the Empire." These words fell like the shadow of an austere, unfamiliar sanctuary between her and me.

"Do you know what the Empire means?" I did not dare answer—then nothing more was spoken.

From that day on, Reverend Mother, I thought only of how I could flee to Valladolid. I no longer wept in my sleep at night but instead jumped in my dreams onto a small, swift Arabian horse and rode through the darkened land. It was the same small, swift horse that I had once ridden in the imperial hunts.—You know, Reverend Mother, I was an impetuous rider; they used to say at court that I rode like a boy. This small, swift horse came each night by magical paths and burst into my chamber and stamped with his hoof on my bedstead. He still carried the same richly ornamented saddle that had once been my childish delight, and soon I was sitting on it and galloping through the dank, foggy night from Flanders, mile after mile, back along the same road by which the Regent's carriage had once brought me. But then at dawn, as I trotted along the road to Salamanca toward Valladolid and saw the high walls of the Castle of Simancas looming ahead of me, then suddenly everything around me became so pale and wan, and then when I had arrived at the gate of the castle, a man stood there whose face already was no longer recognizable, who asked me: Do you too know what the Empire means? And I had to turn back in silence, because in fact I did not know. But when I awoke, I no longer knew why I had turned around, nor did I want to know it, but instead I considered all day long how I could begin to make my dream come true. This, Reverend Mother, is how it must be with the birds when they are drawn forcibly across the sea, or with the plants, when in the spring the sap stirs in them, so that their tender shoots push through the hard crust of the earth. And so they found me one morning before the dew and the dawn lying beneath a green tree several miles distant from Malines and brought me back to the court of the Lady Regent. There the Countess Croy asked me first how I had come to be beneath that green tree. I could find no other explanation but to say that the little Arabian horse had thrown me off there. At that the Countess said to me: "We will have to lock you in at night, Arabella, if you take your dreams so seriously that you run after them into the dark night."

Then the Lady Regent sent for me. Before I went to see her, the Countess Croy said: "Pull yourself together, Arabella; Her Highness has had certain worries recently, and you must not increase them through your willfulness." I did not take this to heart at all, however, because since my last conversation with the Lady Regent, I had again buried myself entirely in my anger against her, because she was unwilling to grant my request to send me to Valladolid.

As I entered her room, she was once again holding the mysterious little girl on her lap. Nearby stood the vain old nurse, her whole face beaming, as though her darling were sitting on the throne that belonged to her. When the Lady Regent caught sight of me, she let the child slip down to the ground, kissed her, and told the nurse to take her out—the child resisted but followed. As she passed by, she sized me up with a defiant look, as if to say: How dare you drive me away? It seemed to me, however, as though my fear of the child had a definite name for the first time. Meanwhile, the Lady Regent was speaking to me.

I had expected that she would scold me, as the Countess Croy had done, on account of my flight. But she only said casually and almost jokingly: "Arabella, I have heard that at night you set out on little Arabian horses and in the morning are found under green trees. And I know, too where the road led—is it still not clear to you, then, what the Empire means?"

While she spoke, the voice of the mysterious little girl could be heard outside the door as the nurse tried in vain to reason with her. Now the child flung the door open and was about to dash back to the Lady Regent. But the latter looked sternly at her and said, "Shame on you, *ma petite!* Have you entirely forgotten, then, who you are?" Now the little girl's face went pale. She drew back, ashamed, fighting off tears, but I also heard how the old nurse at the doorway whispered to her: "Be quiet, sweetheart, you are still the daughter of the beautiful Johanna van der Gheenst!"

When the child had gone out, the Lady Regent adroitly continued speaking to me: "The Empire, Arabella, is the power that humbles the Emperor himself, first of all—he must not allow the slightest reproach to fall upon the one who holds that power. Do you finally understand what I mean?"

I said nothing, choked by a storm of fear and jealousy. Suddenly I heard myself say, "And who is Johanna van der Gheenst?" It sounded as though someone had torn the question from my lips by force. Immediately afterward I knew that I had demanded my own death sentence. And the Lady Regent was already pronouncing it. "Johanna van der Gheenst", she said calmly, "is the mother of the little girl who was just with me. She was born as the Emperor's daughter before there was an empress at court. Since there has been an empress at court, no longer can a Johanna van der Gheenst be there. Do you finally understand now that the Empire humbles the Emperor first of all?" She said this very gravely—almost unapproachably —but then she concluded very kindly again: "Be consoled, my child; you are not suffering alone, therefore."

But I was by no means consoled; no, Reverend Mother, it was no consolation to me. After all, I was enchanted, and no one can help the enchanted, but instead everything helps the enchantment. I had demanded and received the death sentence on my love, but I did not die of it, for love cannot die—again and again, it finds a way to escape death. Of all that the Regent had said, only one thing had actually sunk in: that now in Valladolid there was no longer a Johanna van der Gheenst. And that was enough to let me breathe freely. Yes, Reverend Mother, I was an enchanted woman, almost a possessed woman! Had I not actually been locked in every night by the Countess Croy, I would not have needed my dream pony to attempt a second flight. But for another reason that would not happen again.

Several days later, the Countess Croy informed me that I should make ready to accompany the Lady Regent on a journey. "Her Highness thinks that you need some special diversion", she said with visible reluctance. "Do you realize what a lofty distinction is being granted to you?" Where the journey would end, the Countess Croy did not say, and I would rather have bitten off my tongue than to ask about it. It mattered not at all to me, either —every place was indifferent to me if its name was not Valladolid!

In the next few days the Lady Regent issued several administrative documents with great dispatch and had others postponed until later, among them also the answers to various letters from the imperial chancery that had arrived recently in rapid succession. Meanwhile, all sorts of rumors started about the planned journey. No one knew anything about its destination, after all, except the councilors and the Countess Croy. Naturally the attendants of Her Highness did not want to admit this; they carried their little heads with their lace veils very high, as before, and put on airs of great importance.

"His Majesty needs Her Highness' help", I heard them whispering. Now I was all ears. The question escaped my lips: "Is her Highness traveling to Valladolid, then?"

The ladies smiled mysteriously. "Yes, where else would Her Highness be traveling? No one talks about it, but everyone knows anyway."

Now I was simply blissful—I was so happy that it almost hurt. This will not surprise you anymore, Reverend Mother, since you already know that I was an enchanted woman! Now it mattered to me not at all if the Countess Croy locked me in at night—I sang and laughed in my prison; indeed sometimes a shout of joy escaped me while I was still on the stairs, because I thought I had noticed that the Countess Croy suddenly paid scarcely any attention to etiquette, over which she otherwise kept such a strict watch. Whereas until recently they could joke that she had determined when Her Highness' little dog was and was not allowed to bark and that now it had to walk backward out the door in the presence of royalty—now she overlooked every *faux pas* at court. It was almost as though she had become nearsighted with regard to etiquette, while with respect to the Regent, she seemed to have become farsighted, as though a secret calamity were awaiting her somewhere in the distance.

"If only Her Highness had not dismissed the Roman prelate so quickly then", I heard her lament to Monsieur Des Barres. "I fear, alas, I fear very much . . . ! My one consolation is that Her Highness can rely on His Majesty, as though he were her own son." Once again I was all ears, for they were talking about His Majesty.

"Yes, Her Highness can rely at all times on the filial attitude of His Majesty," Monsieur Des Barres replied, "but this son is, after all, the Emperor as well, and the Emperor is the *defensor ecclesiae*."

This answer seemed to frighten the old Countess. "His Majesty, though, is still not yet reconciled with His Holiness", she objected—it was as if she were fleeing from the thought that Monsieur Des Barres had expressed.

"Certainly," he replied, "but His Majesty will be reconciled. This is about the unity of Christendom. The heresy in Germany demands a council, and for its sake His Majesty will make any sacrifice, but he will also demand the same." Then, significantly: "The Lady Regent intended to raise an emperor, and she did raise an emperor."

After this conversation, the Countess Croy was even

more uneasy and distracted than before; indeed, she was so distracted that one morning she completely forgot to open up the room in which she had been locking me every night since my flight. I was happy about that quiet day and had sweet dreams about the journey to Valladolid, so that I felt neither hunger nor thirst. I also kept very quiet, so that no one noticed my prison. Not until late evening did the Countess become aware of her oversight, after the whole court had already been convinced that I had escaped again. Meanwhile the Regent had ordered that when I was found I was to be brought to her immediately.

She was already in her nightgown and barefoot, sitting in front of her mirror. The chambermaid had just finished combing her hair: it hung like a heavy golden cloak over her shoulders and back—for the first time, I saw her without a widow's veil. I had not spoken to her since our last conversation, and she seemed to me completely changed, as though with her magnificent garments she had also cast off the Princess and the Regent: she looked almost like a young maiden; no, actually, she looked like a bride. There was something expectant about her, something joyfully anxious and yet bold and blissful; yes, Reverend Mother, she must have looked just like that on her wedding day! But my mood, too, was as expectant and joyfully anxious as a bride's, for soon now I was to travel with Her Highness to Valladolid! She noticed my joy and said, "My poor little prisoner, in the future, my good Croy will no longer have to lock you in; I will watch over you myself. You know, do you not, that you are to accompany me on my journey? Are you finally content with me now?" I kissed her hand, for God knows that I was! Even the whippet noticed my joyful demeanor; it jumped up at me as impetuously as if that little courtly animal, too, had already grasped the fact that the Countess Croy was no longer keeping an eye on questions of etiquette.

While I was laughing and warding off the dog, hoofbeats resounded below in the courtyard. The Regent listened, visibly alarmed. A few minutes later, a letter was brought to her: I recognized the imperial seal, and this was the seal of His Majesty himself, not that of the chancery. The Regent was alarmed again; she immediately opened the letter but because of her poor eyesight could not decipher it. "Quickly, quickly, read it to me", she urged, handing it to me. I felt how her hand was trembling, and mine was shaking, too. So now I really was holding in my hand one of those letters that once before I had tried in vain to wrest from the courier. I saw the compact, dignified, and yet utterly straightforward handwriting of His Majesty, I saw the familiar, proud signature: "I, the Emperor". For a moment my eyes, too, seemed to fail— it was a miracle that my voice did not break. I read:

Madame, très chère tante et mère!

The gentle yet deep wisdom of a woman is what convinced me during those days in Cambrai that the self-restraint of the victor is his real and ultimately decisive victory. I do not say the clemency and magnanimity of the victor, for the sober experiences of a ruler make these words difficult to tolerate. It was simply a matter of common sense. The same wisdom that at Cambrai demanded a sacrificial peace with France on account of the danger from the Turks today, for the sake of the unity of Christendom, demands atonement for the *Sacco di Roma*. I have conceded the difficult demands of His Holiness concerning the restoration of the Medicis in Florence as well as the no less difficult stipulations of the Holy See with regard to Parma, Piacenza, and Milan. There still remains the minor wish of the Holy Father, which nevertheless was proposed to me expressly, concerning the church in Brou. Compliance with that wish was promised also. Hence it is incumbent on me to request that Your Highness be so kind as to call off the journey that you have planned and not to set foot in Brou until your work has complied with the wishes of His Holiness. I recommend that Your Highness take at once the steps necessary for this. I know very well that with this communication I am causing you great sorrow. It goes against my childlike feelings to utter a command in your regard, but I do not hide the fact that I would have to utter a command if you were unable to command yourself. Allow me therefore to conclude with that difficult but mighty phrase which you once recommended to me as a motto, when my duty was to struggle for the victory of Cambrai: *Plus ultra*.

I, the Emperor

When I had finished, the Regent sat there as though completely numb. Suddenly she jumped up, snatched the letter from me, and crumpled it in her hand. "Send me the Countess", she ordered, pronouncing her words posthaste. "We will set out for Brou tomorrow before dawn."

"For Brou, Your Highness," I stammered, "for Brou? But we were supposed to go to Valladolid!"

"No, we intended to go to Brou", she replied severely.

"I want to visit my husband! Send for the Countess!"

I felt a horrible pain. Motionless, incapable of carrying out her order, I remained standing there. Slowly in her agitation she comprehended my disappointment. "Foolish child," she said half angrily, half compassionately, "so you are still unwilling to understand what the Empire is! You have still not bowed down before it!" She paused and looked at me almost in alarm: out of the dreadful disappointment within me arose the upright candle flame of an abysmal triumph, for she, too, was unwilling to understand what the Empire means; she, too, did not want to bow down before it! I might have thrown this accusation in her face, but she had already understood it. Completely calm and utterly majestic, she said: "So, Arabella, now give me the sleeping potion, too, and then send for the Countess Croy." It sounded as though nothing had happened. An immense desire to humiliate her overcame me, to bend that proud head to the same yoke that she wanted to force on mine. With a trembling hand, I grabbed the ruby-glass goblet, the precious gift from the Emperor, which the chambermaid had already filled, and now I was completely and utterly swept away: I did not decide to do what happened next, but it just happened. I raised the imperial glass goblet and lifted it high, as though I were drinking to her. *"Plus ultra!"* I said in a resounding voice. I then saw her become deathly pale; felt how she snatched the goblet out of my hand—and the next moment it clattered to the floor.

I think that she then dismissed me—I still remember that I went to the door without a word, but before I reached it, I heard a faint scream. Turning around, I saw her face distorted by a great physical pain. Blood was trickling on the floor—she had cut her bare foot on a shard from the broken goblet.

And now, Reverend Mother: you know what the whole world knows, I mean the distressing end of the Lady Regent, which was caused by a wound that was seemingly so insignificant and so accidental for someone of her station. The next day the Lady Regent could not rise, nor the day after that. On the third day, a severe wound-fever set in, and the doctors helplessly observed its virulent course. Soon it was no secret that gangrene had affected the injured limb and threatened to poison the whole body. Do not ask me to describe my own state! I had alternately loved and hated the Lady Regent; now I knew that at bottom even my hatred had been love. I cried my eyes out when I thought about her sufferings—after all, it was my exclamation that had caused her anger to run over. The wish that had prompted me had been fulfilled: she had felt that she, too, was unwilling to bow down to the Empire, but she had to pay for it with her life! A profound and quite helpless remorse filled me; alas, I was facing remorse for the first time—I did not know how I was supposed to deal with it! For several days it drove every other feeling from my heart, even my yearning for Valladolid. Often I stole after the Countess Croy when she was about to hurry into the sickroom with bandages and ointments; I had only one wish, to be allowed to follow her, so that I could ask Her Highness for forgiveness. But the Countess paid no attention to me, no one did; they were all filled with their sorrow and care about the sick woman. Only the haughty little daughter of the beautiful Johanna van der Gheenst, who now was just as abandoned as I, occasionally threw her arms around my neck when she met me in the empty halls and chambers of the Regency, and then we wept together like two children who had always been on good terms with each other.

On the seventh day, I heard a scratching at my door. When I opened it, Her Highness' whippet stood there in front of me and looked at me with its sad dog eyes. I fell to my knees and wept into its little silken coat. It wriggled loose in a refined, solemn way, almost reproachfully, and slowly walked back the way that it had come, turning back toward me again and again, as if it were trying to bid me to follow. I did, and it led me down the stairs and across to the Regency. There it stopped outside Her Highness' bedroom and scratched again. I opened the door for it, and it slipped inside and approached the Regent's bed, the curtains of which had been drawn back. I could not see her, though, because her councilors stood gathered around the bed; her notary was present, too. I heard her dictating a letter. As I appeared, two chambermaids stood up from the foot of the bed and tried to send me away. The Lady Regent stopped in mid-sentence and said in a weak but very clear voice: "I have been expecting Arabella; I would like her to stay." Then she continued dictating: "The hour has come, Sire, for me to make ready to accept the last thing from God's hand. With my conscience at ease, the only sorrow I feel now is that I will not have the privilege of beholding Your Majesty again in this life. I leave to Your Majesty as my sole heir the land entrusted to me, returning it not only intact, but also augmented in honor and wealth after a regency for which I hope to receive God's reward and Your Majesty's thanks. I recommend once again to Your Majesty peace, especially with the King of France. I commend to Your Majesty all my faithful servants and maidservants. I commend to you finally the beloved church in Brou as the resting place of my dear husband, at whose side I myself wish to be laid to rest. I therefore beg Your Majesty as a final favor . . ."

She was about to add something else, but her strength suddenly abandoned her. She was completely silent for several minutes, during which the chambermaids who were present sought to revive her with smelling salts. Then, coming to her senses again but still very weak, she added only these words softly:

". . . with this fervent request I bid Your Majesty farewell in this world."

They handed the document to the Lady Regent for her signature. Then the councilors, profoundly moved, reverently kissed her hand and left the room. I could see the bed clearly. The Lady Regent, exhausted, had now shut her eyes. Her hair was undone, and her face appeared to have sunk down in the middle of it. She had her hands folded—now she looked as she does on her tombstone. The whippet had snuggled at her feet, as though it wanted to die at the same time as its mistress—and in fact this faithful little animal survived her only by a few days.— A few minutes passed in this way; then the Regent opened her eyes again and said in a clear voice that had become even fainter: "Now I want to bid farewell to my ladies individually. Allow me to begin with the youngest."

Now everyone present went outside, Reverend Mother, and it seemed miraculous to me that they did so and that I was allowed to remain alone with the dying woman. But probably no one had the courage to contradict her last orders. I fell to my knees beside her bed. "O Madame," I sobbed, "Madame, I have killed you! Had I remained silent when I handed you the goblet, you could now travel to Brou to visit your husband!"

She whispered: "Not you; the Emperor handed me this cup—he had to do it, his high office demanded it. I am dying because I did not drink this cup willingly, but I die willingly. No, do not blame yourself, my child; you only helped me to push open a door, for now I am allowed to travel to Brou after all; even the Emperor will no longer raise an objection to it. I will be united with my husband and never again leave him."

While she spoke, her face had become increasingly transfigured—despite all the shadows of death that lay over it, a joy broke through that seemed to me not at all of this world. Again she appeared to me like a bride on her wedding day, no, like a saint on the day of her death. All at once I could no longer tell: Was she speaking about the tomb in the church in Brou or about the bliss of heaven; did she mean being laid to rest in the grave at her husband's side or entering into God's rest? Quite suddenly the last words she had spoken then to the prelate came to my mind.

She smiled at me in a strangely knowing manner. (Reverend Mother, they do say that the dying are clairvoyant!) "Yes, wild little Arabella," she whispered, "yes, my confidence in love has not betrayed me. God has enlarged my heart in dying—if I could, I would now build the altar for him, but the Emperor will do it for me—I requested it of him as a final favor. Now all that is left for me is to open the door for you—for know, child, that in all eternity there is only one love that comes from heaven, even though this world calls it earthly—God accepts it as though it were offered to him personally . . ." At these last words, her voice took on the tone of someone who was quietly slipping away. The color of her face changed, too, as though an otherworldly joy were already concealing her features. (Reverend Mother, never did a human being die as blessedly as the Lady Regent!) She whispered once again: "Yes, I love God . . . I love him . . . I have loved him from of old . . . I loved him in his likeness . . ." Right after that, she sank into a deep swoon. You know, Reverend Mother, that she never again awoke from it into consciousness.

I will leave out now the long, painful ceremonies that followed the passing of the Lady Regent and the initial preparations to dissolve her former royal household. At that time, most of the ladies of Her Highness decided to return to their families; others were to be taken in by the court of the Empress, and still others by the Archduchess Marie, the widowed Queen of Hungary, who, as was reported, had been designated by His Majesty as the successor of Her Highness. Even the little daughter of the beautiful Johanna van der Gheenst left the old ducal court then so as to be entrusted to a Spanish noblewoman for her upbringing. Only my future seemed to remain untouched by the changes. I had no family into whose bosom I could return, and no one ever said that I should be taken in by the Empress or recommended to the Archduchess Marie; instead, it seemed, now that the Lady Regent was no more, that I was something of an embarrassment for everyone. It is true that the Countess Croy looked after me now in a very motherly way; this was an expression of her great love for the Lady Regent, which she demonstrated to her beyond the grave because she had been so affectionately devoted to me. And this was certainly not easy for the Countess Croy to do, for personally she was by no means well-disposed toward me. Nor could she forgive me for being the one who had had the privilege of hearing the last words of Her Highness, especially since I jealously withheld these words from her and from everyone else, since they were all too closely connected with my own fate. Finally, though, the Countess Croy did come up with a plan for me: she told me that it would probably be best if I entered a convent. I naturally resisted like a little animal that someone is trying to drown. She held her tongue and sighed, but she returned again and again to the idea; indeed, she urged me with painful persistence, and soon I was to learn why. At around the same time when the Countess Croy began to recommend the convent to me, news spread at the court that the Emperor was coming to Malines in order to settle personally several items of business that had been left unfinished by the decease of Her Highness, before Queen Marie took over.

You will probably think, Reverend Mother, that the Lady Regent's death and the pain of remorse had transformed me interiorly. Alas, no, nothing about me had changed! The black crêpe of mourning and that pain of remorse had merely covered my passion for a little while. Now it burst forth twice as strong: the Emperor was coming to Malines; I no longer needed to flee to Valladolid; Valladolid would be in Malines . . . at last I was to meet the look of love that I yearned for so ardently . . . at last I was to give an answer to the unrequited! The Countess Croy now spoke not another word about the convent . . . the courage to do so probably failed her at the sight of my beaming face, however odd it may have looked beneath my mourning veil. Ah, the poor Countess Croy, how she must have despaired of me! She gave no sign of it, however, but instead repeatedly ordered me in those days to accompany her to the chapel of the Sisters of the Annunciation Order, to whom the Lady Regent's mortal remains had been entrusted until the church in Brou was ready to receive them. We knelt there together, praying beside her silent sarcophagus and laid flowers on it; then we went back to the Regency.

Now one day, when we were finished with our usual prayers, the Countess murmured to me that I should stay a little longer with our dead Mistress while she herself called on the Lady Prioress. I did as she told me, and she went but never came back. After a while, instead of her, a gentle young nun appeared, took me amicably by the hand, and led me, not to the waiting Countess as I supposed, but to the Prioress. The latter informed me just as gently and amicably that I had become for a while the dear guest of her and her sisters—I would not have to stay for too long a time; they would do everything they could to shorten it.

Of course, I understood right away that I was a prisoner—it was only a few days before the arrival of His Majesty. I was a prisoner, someone being held gently, amicably, but relentlessly in custody. The barred windows of the house, the awareness of the strictly locked gates of the monastic enclosure left no doubt: they wanted to set me aside while His Majesty was present in Malines. Of all the disappointments that I already called my own, this was the cruelest and most distressing. In vain I shook the window grating at night until my hands sank down in pain and my eyelids drooped in exhaustion—not even my little dream horse succeeded in breaking through the religious devotion of those walls, which was all too strange to him. Only a miracle could have unlocked my prison. Meanwhile, the Emperor entered Malines.

And now the miracle happened! Several days later, the Countess Croy stood in front of me in the convent parlor. Now, Reverend Mother, I had been prudent and proud enough not to let my pious jailers notice my indignation over my involuntary stay in their house. For, in the first place, those good, worldly-unwise women most probably could not help having been saddled with me, and, secondly, I knew from past experience that with my tears I would only achieve more stringent supervision. In silence

I had complied with all the rules of the daily horarium in the cloister. I suspect the good sisters went on with their lives thinking I felt completely at ease among them. But at the sight of the Countess Croy, my haughty disguise broke down: without greeting her, I buried my head in both hands to show her my contempt on account of her deceit. Gently but firmly she pulled my hands away from my face and said, "Look me in the eyes, dear child, I come on account of a request of His Majesty." Then she informed me that the Emperor had expressed the desire to speak with the lady who had been the only one present at the last words of his *très chère tante et mère*. I do not know what I said in reply, no, I really do not know! It was as though an earthquake shook my soul, so that all the stones flew from the tombs of my hope: The Emperor desired to hear the Regent's last words . . . no one could comply with his request except me . . . I would see him again . . . I would in spite of everything . . . he himself, the Emperor, would request it!

Suddenly I heard the Countess Croy say: "No, you misunderstand me, Arabella. We cannot allow this conversation, because there is no one at court who does not know why you once had to leave Valladolid. Even the Emperor will not insist on this conversation once he learns the name of that lady. Will you at last confide to me the last words of Her Highness, so that I can convey them in your place?"

Instantly I said, "No, I will not." And I stood by it, because I felt that consequently I held a talisman in my hands. She sought to wrest it from my grasp, but I held fast. I repeated triumphantly in response to all her urging that I would give an account to the Emperor himself and to him alone.

The Countess was desperate. "But understand, my child," she begged, "this is not about you; it is about the inviolability of His Majesty. Alas, if only you had followed my advice and entered the convent!"

Now an audacious idea occurred to me. "As someone who has entered the convent, would I be allowed to speak with His Majesty?" I asked.

She replied hesitantly: Such a vow would of course silence many rumors, and indeed I myself knew that the imperial desire had been along those lines already in Valladolid.

And now, Reverend Mother, you would be right to expect that a struggle began within me. But there was nothing of the sort—not for one moment did I struggle with myself, not one! From the outset I had made my decision unquestionably. Across from me shimmered a narrow old mirror on the wall, which the good nuns had permitted in this cloistered room for the sake of their guest's youthful vanity. I can still see my deceitful little face clearly in the shiny glass as I told the poor Countess bluntly that I had decided to follow her advice. Indeed, I was wily enough to maintain that my stay with these good cloistered nuns had won me over to the religious state—without batting an eyelash, I declared that I was ready to confirm this by taking a vow immediately.

Her eyes became big and round, but she did not dismiss my suggestion—was I deceiving her, or was she willing to be deceived? Alas, long ago she had stopped sleeping

with her eyes open—since the Regent's death she really
had become a blind old woman. Then, too, she had ardently yearned for me to take this vow—in short, she
believed me. Later I heard that she was backed by others,
for whom my pretended decision at that moment was unquestionably opportune. And so they accepted my vow:
I solemnly committed myself to life in a religious order,
although I had no intention whatsoever of keeping this
promise; instead, I did what I did solely in order to obtain the meeting with the Emperor. In doing so, I had
no other thought than to requite that look of love which
once rested upon me. Beyond that aim, there was nothing
whatsoever left for me. My vow was therefore a complete
fraud, indeed, a sacrilege, and I have no other excuse for
it than the inexcusable willingness of those who allowed
that headlong act—alas, they were only too glad on account of it! A few days later, the Countess Croy accompanied me back to the Regency, where in the former audience chamber of Her Highness my interview with His
Majesty was to take place.

As I entered, a slender, masculine figure stood up and
took a few steps toward me. I heard a slightly muted
voice: "Donna Arabella, allow Us to show you the honor
befitting your future state." I found myself being led to
an armchair and was invited to take a seat. The Emperor
sat down opposite me on the Regent's chair. But I could
not recognize his face—I was like someone who had suddenly gone blind. I had not understood the meaning of the
Emperor's words, either—the rapture of being near him
robbed me of all my strength. I only knew that the look

for which I had almost pined away must now be falling on me. Trembling, I lifted mine and felt all the desire, all the ardor, and all the devotion of my soul rush to my eyes, offering themselves to the other's eyes, giving themselves blissfully, unconditionally, and unreservedly. I felt this for only a few seconds . . . then my gaze tottered back . . . I had recognized the face in front of me. But how unspeakably changed it was . . . how much had dwindled in that face, oh, how much in it had dwindled away in those few years of his reign! To be sure, it was still that pale, noble face with the slightly protruding lower lip, disturbingly young—much too disturbingly young for an emperor—and still disturbingly lonely, too! But this loneliness no longer resembled an open door that challenges one to enter. It had, so to speak, turned in on itself; it had been taken in by its own depth, taken in and transformed, just as a delicate, wistful landscape can be transformed into a heroic one when out of the stones on its hills one builds a castle whose walls loom high over the natural terrain. No trembling of the slender hand that rested on the arm of the lofty chair, no twitch of the blond eyelashes betrayed any agitation of memory, and no look, either— that summoning look about which I had dreamed day and night that I must somehow answer it—that look was no longer there; there was only the look of the Emperor. I was confronted with sheer inaccessibility, pure Majesty. It was as though I were falling into an abyss. For the first time I understood what the Empire means.

Meanwhile, the muted voice was speaking to me a second time: "Donna Arabella, We congratulate you on your decision to take the veil. The Christian West is presently in dire straits and requires many prayers. We gratefully take this opportunity to commend Ourselves and Our Realm to yours." Once again I felt as though swallowed up by a pit: the Emperor really believed, therefore, that I wanted to take the veil, and he had to believe it—I had shamefully deceived him as I had all the others by lying. In my madness, I had not yet been aware of that. But now within me the illusions fell like fog—a burning shame overcame me, a feeling of the most profound unworthiness before the guilelessness of this young ruler: the pain caused by his coolness still seemed to be a kindness in comparison with his contempt. And yet, I felt, the latter was unavoidable if my imposture came to light. There was only one escape: I had to make the lie true, I had to believe in my vow, I had to keep it. But how dreadful that was! Ah, the cool, dead air of these convent rooms! Ah, these unceasing prayers and spiritual exercises, day and night! Ah, to be buried alive like this! Who was to grant me the strength for that? No one was there but an emperor—I had nothing to hearten me for the ordeal except sheer Majesty. Meanwhile, he was waiting for an answer—I had to make a decision. A reckless despair came over me: yes, there was no one there but an emperor, but would it not be possible to love even an emperor? Could it not be done even behind cloister walls? Yes, it was possible—this was where the majesty of one's own heart began—here I was of equal birth! And I wanted to be so.

"Not only my prayers, but my whole future religious life shall be a continual sacrifice for Your Majesty and Your Majesty's reign . . ." It was settled, I had repeated

my vow, and this time it was irrevocable, this time it was
a perpetual vow; I would have to stand by it until the end
of my life!

The Emperor was silent. Had the vehemence in my answer disconcerted him? The young lonely face in front
of me remained inscrutable. And now the figure no
longer was leaning back slightly but straightened up—
quite abruptly His Majesty got to the real purpose of the
interview. I heard the question: "Have We been correctly
informed, Donna Arabella, that you were already present
when the Lady Regent was dictating that farewell letter
to us, which concluded with the request that We should
take care of her work, the church in Brou?"

I replied that that was the case. The Emperor hesitated
an instant, as though he were seeking another expression not immediately at his disposal—in this hesitation
there was something very refined—I understood that he
wanted to protect the dead woman's secret. Finally, he
said almost precipitously, "We wish, therefore, above all
to know what Her Highness meant by that request, since
a sentence was missing in her letter. What impression did
you have of the last moments of Her Highness?"

I replied, "Her Highness seemed to me like a dying
saint."

The Emperor looked up in joyful surprise, but immediately lowered his glance again before it met mine.
"You think, therefore," he said, "that you understood
Her Highness to mean, that in one point"—the muted
voice once again sought an impartial expression—"in one
extremely important point she had submitted to God's de-

mands?'' There was an uneasy tension in the young Emperor's voice, which no doubt concerned the salvation of his beloved relative's soul.

I was unable to answer immediately. Had the last words of Her Highness then really signified the submission that the Emperor meant? Did they not represent at the same time, in fact did they not represent above all the total victory of her love? But the Emperor was asking about submission. I had to think back to them first.—Imagine, Reverend Mother: this, of all things, had not occurred to your self-willed child.

"Her Highness", I said tentatively, "expressed the hope that the church in Brou would receive through Your Majesty's good offices the high altar that it still lacks."

"This was what I hoped to learn from you", the Emperor said, visibly relieved. "I thank you. You have given me the certainty that Her Highness departed from this world as a Christian princess and an emperor's daughter. And now, Donna Arabella, may your own departure from the world be a sacrifice offered to the pure love of God . . ." The Emperor made a gesture to dismiss me.

A crippling dread seized me: Was this all that I had purchased with my terrible vow? Was I to be buried all my life for this paltry conversation? Once again the ardent, desperate passion sprang up. Yes, there was no one there but an emperor, and one could love an emperor, but even an emperor could feel that there is such a thing as majesty of the heart, and he should feel it.

"Sire," I said, beside myself, "the last words of Her Highness were: 'I love God, I have loved him from of old, I loved him in his likeness—for there is only one love . . . God accepts every love as though it were offered to him personally.' " And now my eyes did plunge into that long since preoccupied look, to requite which had seemed to me to be the only meaning of my life—for the first time my immense agitation allowed me to look at the Emperor wide-eyed. At my words, he had gone extremely pale, the impressive self-control in his young face wavered and gave way to a fatal horror: I had given an answer to that look from the past, and the answer had been understood. A man had grasped what sort of love my vow signified. Breathless, bottomless silence threatened to engulf everything—but now the Emperor once again stood up. Still extraordinarily pale, he offered me his arm. I was led to the door chivalrously, and there the strictly ceremonial farewell took place in complete silence. I believed that that silence could never again be broken.

And yet it was to be broken. Several days later the imperial confessor appeared in the convent of the Sisters of the Annunciation, to which the Countess Croy had taken me back immediately after the audience. With courteous levity, in which there was an undertone of paternal benevolence, he informed me that His Majesty had had the impression that my vow to enter religious life had been made in circumstances contrary to the requirement of complete interior freedom. His Majesty therefore offered to apply in Rome for a dispensation from my vow and to make it possible for me to return to the world, either as a court attendant in the retinue of a noblewoman or through an adoption into an aristocratic family in my homeland. A suitable marriage, if I should desire that, could also be considered.

At that I winced vehemently, and the priest tactfully stopped short. The choice among these suggestions, he then continued, was left up to me. In making them, His Majesty wanted nothing else but to restore to me complete freedom about my future life. "Take heart, therefore, Donna Arabella," he concluded, "and do not be afraid to correct a wrong decision. Set out with confidence on the path that His Majesty intends to clear for you—it is the appropriate one for you."

But now something amazing came about: I was unable to set out on that path. What had happened? Had I not just been shuddering with the utmost dread and horror at the life of a cloistered nun? Had I not returned from the audience with the awareness: Now this life is over, now comes the long night? And instead, now they were saying: No, now comes a new day! I was to jump again into the richly ornamented saddle of a little Arabian horse; I was to be allowed to dance, play the lute, and use cosmetics—I was to wear a wreath in my hair and a ring on my finger like other brides—I was supposed to, I was allowed to, and yet it no longer meant anything to me! It had lost its meaning and attraction. The world suddenly lay as though submerged behind me—only one thing had meaning now. The Emperor was the one who was giving me back my lost freedom—everyone else had been intent only on obligating it. Everyone else had seen in me only the child lacking in comprehension; he cared for me as someone of equal birth, as someone worthy of freedom.

He had at one time wanted to send the dreamer off to the convent; to the awakened lover he showed the reverence of letting her decide. I felt, indeed, that this was the greatest thing he could bestow on me. Yes, my life was starting over, but precisely at the place where hitherto I thought it had ended, for now I could live only for the Emperor, and where could I do that outside of convent walls?

"Monseigneur," I said, beaming, "convey to His Majesty my thanks for his generous gift. I have chosen again. In complete freedom I repeat the answer that I have already given to His Majesty: my future religious life shall be a continual sacrifice for His Majesty and His Majesty's reign."

The father confessor looked at me searchingly for a long time. He had an unconvinced but not incredulous facial expression—a lot of knowledge about human beings and a lot of doubt about them seemed to be engraved on it, but there was nothing petty in that countenance.

"I will not try to persuade you otherwise, Donna Arabella," he finally said, "for that would be pointless. I know that even earthly love can be a path to God, as the great Plato once taught. The imperial government needs interceding helpers, for the course of the world is not determined by man alone. Dedicate yourself, therefore, to pleading for His Majesty in the presence of God. I will convey your decision—whether His Majesty will accept it, I do not know. Expect no answer."

Then he gave me his blessing and went away.

What I have yet to write down is known to you, Reverend Mother, in its main outlines. Almost immediately after the conversation recorded above, I entered the Order of the Sisters of the Annunciation, to whose protection, as I have already said, the mortal remains of the Lady Regent had been entrusted until their transport to Brou. When this happened, I already wore the novice's veil, and the Rule of the Order therefore did not allow me to leave the cloister. But something extremely unusual happened: I was surprised to receive permission from my superiors to accompany those dear remains to Brou. You yourself, Reverend Mother, who were visiting the convent in those same days as our General Superior, brought me the bishop's dispensation. No doubt it had been issued at the request of someone higher up, although the only reason stated was that it befitted the dignity of the departed noblewoman to be accompanied not only by representatives of the estates of the land, led by Count Hogstraten, but also by one of her ladies, and in particular by the one whom she had appointed during her lifetime as her companion on the journey to Brou.

And so I went once again out into the world, in order to share the final, moving journey of my former Mistress.— You have already received, Reverend Mother, the official reports of it.—Upon our arrival in Brou we learned that first the church was to be consecrated, since the high altar donated by His Majesty had already found a place in it. Whereas many high-ranking guests were expected for the funeral, the intention was to carry out the consecration in the greatest silence imaginable in the presence of only the most necessary witnesses—understandably they wanted to conceal from the public the late date of this solemn act, so as not to fuel all over again certain rumors about the Lady Regent. Originally they had expected the Emperor himself in Brou, but reportedly he was tied up with difficult government business and was only able to appoint a representative, whose name was not made known.

Very early in the morning, the Count von Hogstraten and I went to the church; waiting at the entrance were two priests who silently guided us through the nave. It was completely empty; only to one side, where the signs of the cross are located on the exterior walls of a church, the procession of the consecrating bishop and his clergy moved slowly along. We entered the choir, where the two priests showed us our stalls. Mine was lined with red fabric, and a matching pillow lay on the floor. Yet I scarcely paid attention to this finery—I was too deeply moved by the room, which was filled with the love of my dead Mistress—the love that now had reached its perfection in God. I thought about the legacy of the great hour of her death—would it be true someday for me, too: God accepts every love as though it were offered to him personally? Alas, not even the Emperor seemed to accept mine —as the father confessor foretold, he had never answered me. Had my choice been rejected? Did he refuse to allow the prayers and sacrifices of an earthly lover to plead for him in the presence of God? I did not know. But was it necessary to know that? Was not my whole religious life from the start founded on that extreme longing which is not allowed to demand certainty? And was not all truly great love always ready to give gratuitously? No: no certainty was needed and no answer.

Meanwhile, the bishop with his clergy had completed the various acts of consecration. The church had been offered to God, and now God moved into it: Mass began, the first Mass in this house of worship. I knelt down. As I did, my glance was fixed for the first time consciously on the finery decorating my stall—the red velvet with which it was lined displayed the imperial motto. At that it became clear to me that I was occupying the place that had originally been appointed for His Majesty—I was that unnamed representative. Deeply moved, I bent down and kissed the words: *Plus ultra*.

Reverend Mother, I have finished the report that you required of me.

At the Gate of Heaven

IN THE FAMILY ARCHIVE of my mother's relatives there was a curious old document. No one knew how it had actually come to be there or what connection it had with the family. For nowhere in their very carefully recorded annals was there any evidence that one of its members had studied astronomy and natural science in the seventeenth century in Italy, and the provenance of the document refers back to that time, that country, and that discipline. In the family it was called, by quite a stretch of the imagination, the "Galileo Document", although there were no clues whatsoever pointing toward that name. The only certain thing was that the contents revolved around the fate of a typical scholar in those days. Really, the fact that the writer had carefully avoided naming names— obviously for fear of the Inquisition, which at that time vigorously prosecuted supporters of the new natural science—in no way entitled the family to file it together with their own history, except perhaps that on a trip to Italy my cousin Marianne had discovered her own heraldic design among the numerous coats of arms of former students that famously decorate the rooms of the old University of Padua, which of course by no means shed any light on the mystery of the "Galileo Document". Moreover, as is often the case with such old documents, it was held in high honor, to be sure, but almost never read. And so I, too, first became acquainted with its contents on that significant night during the Second World War, when I found myself, at the request of my cousin Marianne, collecting the most important documents in her family archives from the old townhouse where they were stored, so as to bring them to safety from the dangers of the war that threatened them there. Marianne herself, who was spending the war years at my place in the country, had little children and could not easily get away. Her husband, like most of the men in our family, was at the front, and naturally we both had doubts about entrusting this extremely valuable shipment to non-relatives. So then I decided to take charge of it, although well-meaning friends advised against it, since we were affected by the increasing number of air raids on German cities. Yet it is part of human nature, after all, to be able to imagine something unheard-of theoretically but not realistically; moreover, like Marianne, I came from a very old family and was deeply convinced of the importance of my mission—in short, I was rather carefree as I set out on my journey.

The early autumn evening had already set in when I arrived in the city. The railway station seemed strange in the blackout and a little unsettling. It goes without saying that there were no more taxis, so I set out on my way on foot with my little suitcase. Now I saw for the first time a city that had been blacked out: the familiar streets, with their late medieval half-timbered construction, their Baroque palaces and ancient churches, swept here and there in a ghostly fashion by the bluish lights of the very slow-moving streetcars, seemed to me to be masquerading: pitch black windows everywhere, people anxiously fumbling past each other, as if they were hurrying, similarly disguised, to a ghostly carnival. But I personally was also participating in this spooky Mardi Gras. Indeed, it was as though this general masquerade were trying to extend itself even into my interior life—suddenly I no longer knew my way around within myself. It seemed to me quite senseless that I had come to fetch those old documents, which moments before I had regarded as the most precious heritage of the centuries. It seemed inevitable to me that they would perish; indeed, it seemed almost sensible to me, as though this blackout were destined to engulf my whole era and all its traditions. It would not have taken much to persuade me to go back to the railway station without completing my errand, but now I had already reached my destination: I entered my relatives' old townhouse, and inside I was welcomed by an illuminated room and a young man, a distant relative of the family, whom Marianne had asked to help me inspect the archives. I was acquainted with him already from earlier visits; he had earned a doctorate in science with distinction and until now had done military service in the laboratory of an arms factory in the city, but now he faced immediate deployment to the front, which, as he told me, was supposed to take place the next day very early in the morning—hence we had to begin examining the materials right away. I was more than agreeable with that and wondered in relief whether it might be possible for me to shorten my stay there and return to the country by the night train.

The young doctor, to whom I voiced this hope, shrugged his shoulders fatalistically. To say it at the outset: I did not find him sympathetic. Even his way of talking—this extremely free and easy jargon of a younger generation that had not yet found its own language—got on my nerves somewhat. I felt toward this young, self-assured person an odd bashfulness that is otherwise foreign to me, as though suddenly the natural relationship of the generations to each other had been reversed, and I, who was so much older, was in reality the inexperienced one and not competent to judge. In a word, in his presence I felt peculiarly backward and outdated, but at the same time also—an odd contradiction—a little immature, as if experiences of which I had not even the slightest notion stood between us. Yes, to tell the truth, long-forgotten feelings from my teenage years rose up in me, from that age when you would like so much to be taken seriously, while everyone persists in addressing you almost as a child. That is exactly how this young man treated me—quite naïvely, of course, and with a humiliating matter-of-factness. But now was not the time to indulge in such feelings. I now felt completely convinced again of the importance of my task, and so we got down to work.

The young doctor had already prepared the materials, and so the business proceeded relatively quickly. Except that the abundance of the existing documents made for difficulties—good heavens, over several centuries of family history all sorts of things accumulate! And my little suitcase, on which I had to rely to transport them, imposed certain limitations. Therefore, we selected the most important things, and I was about to close the suit-

case when, fortunately, the "Galileo Document" also occurred to me. Marianne, who was filled with a romantic
enthusiasm for it, had recommended it to me very spe-
cially. The young doctor had overlooked it or else had
put it aside as being less important, since it seemed to him
that it did not concern the family, but now he pulled it
out again, as I briefly told him what it was about. At the
name Galileo, he was all ears, cast an interested glance at
the yellowed pages, and then declared that he absolutely
had to read them, too. I reminded him that I wanted to
travel back by the night train.

"Are you afraid that bombs could fall here?" he asked,
without raising his eyes from the manuscript.

"If I were afraid, I certainly would not have come
here", I retorted stiffly. He laughed dispassionately; I felt
he did not believe a word I said. But strangely enough, I
did not believe myself, either. "My train leaves in half an
hour", I repeated somewhat helplessly, "and it is a rather
long manuscript."

"Are you acquainted with it?" he asked, again without
looking up and leafing through the pages. And when I
said no, he said, visibly pleased, "Well, then it is high
time." With that he opened the document to the beginning and began to read aloud to me what I recount here
—for the pages themselves would soon meet their fate.
This, then, was what I heard at that time:

I (three crosses followed in place of the name), a disciple
of the venerable and highly celebrated Master (again three
crosses followed), who have had both the honor and the
affliction of knowing the unspeakable fate of that same

venerable man in all its particulars, to wit, not as the world supposes that it knows it, but rather as it was in truth: I would like to bear witness here to this truth, before myself and before the generations to come. I would like to testify, not only for the Master's sake, but also for the sake of his enemies, or, rather, for the one who was not his enemy and wished not to be his enemy but became and had to become his enemy—I mean, then, the mighty lord who brought about the Master's downfall by falling himself. Nevertheless, I do not want to anticipate these events but rather to report everything faithfully from the beginning.

I begin with that memorable day when the venerable Master had set out on his journey to Rome to justify himself before the ecclesiastical court. We, his students who stayed behind, were still quite calm then: indeed, as is often the case with youth, almost arrogantly confident in the superiority and unassailability of our Master, but also confident in that mighty lord in Rome, whom we were accustomed to address as the patron and protector of our young science. I still remember how we presumed to make the most casual jokes about the lords of the ecclesiastical tribunal, because they had dared to summon the Master before their judgment seat, and if we had any anxiety about the latter, it concerned only the inconveniences of the journey for the already gray-haired traveler or the notorious nuisance of banditry on the roads of the papal states, which since the departure of stern Pope Sixtus had regained the upper hand. Only after we had received news of the Master's safe arrival in Rome was

I first seized with fear for him, yet it was not related to that news but, rather, had an altogether different cause. For on the evening of that day, Diana, the maiden whom I adored, who was privileged to call herself the niece and disciple of our Master, came to me for the first time in a long while in the lofty room, wide open to the firmament, which we—the Master's disciples—facetiously called the "Gate of Heaven", because it stored the instruments and spyglasses with which the Master taught us to explore the starry sky. I was so startled by the appearance of the object of my adoration that my hands flapped and fluttered, as it were, when I handed her the telescope that she requested. But I thought I noticed a slight trembling in hers as well, although I did not dare to ascribe it to my proximity, for it had never yet occurred to me that she could even perceive my feelings, much less requite them. Alas, to my boyish admiration she was not a female creature like other maidens—to me she was almost a goddess! How wondrous she appeared, if only because of her studies, otherwise so rare among those of her sex! My fellow students jokingly called her Urania, and indeed, to me that sounded like the only name worthy of her, for did she not walk beneath the stars like that heavenly muse? I can still see her, her intelligent, proud face uplifted toward the Master with solemn devotion; only occasionally, when he—by chance or on purpose, I know not—spoke for a long time to her countenance, was it radiant, as though it had assumed some of the gleam of his starry universe. Only in the last few days, as the journey to Rome began to approach, had she often seemed

to me pensive and troubled, and although until then she
had charmed us by the clever, bright questions she asked
the Master—oddly enough, she liked to call him Master
and not Uncle—now she fell completely silent during his
lectures, and I had also noticed that she withdrew often
into the nearby convent of Poor Clare nuns, to pray con-
tinuously for many hours in their chapel.

On the night about which I am speaking, we awaited
the rise of the planet Jupiter and of its four moons, those
famous "Medici stars" which, according to the recent
great discoveries, revolved around it and on account of
which my German master had sent me to Italy, so that we
could determine their significance for the position of the
earth in the universe. Although I had not been in Italy
for long, I had already seen those stars several times, but
always veiled, for during the latter days, while the Master was still fighting to avoid a journey to Rome, the sky
had been constantly overcast. Now, after the decision had
been made, it suddenly appeared preternaturally clear, so
that we could expect the most magnificent view of the
planet. And so it rose up in triumph, beaming, as befits a
regal heavenly body, accompanied by its satellites, those
same "Medici stars" that I now perceived with complete
clarity for the first time. It seemed as though the sky itself
wanted to bear witness to the Master: I had never felt so
captivated by the truth thereof as on that night—or did
the nearness of the maiden whom I adored heighten the
receptivity of my mind and of my senses to an intoxicating enthusiasm? I felt that the maiden whom I adored was
overwhelmed, too, by the same enthusiasm: although she
remained motionless at the telescope, I thought I could

hear her heart beating as loudly as mine. Without looking at her, I could tell she was seized by a tremendous
emotion just as I myself was: we felt, thought, and expe-
rienced the very same thing at that moment. To be sure,
we both had long since known what these stars meant,
but we knew it now as never before, in a way that shook
our whole being and nature. This was the moment in
which the old world view finally dissolved for both of
us and shattered in a noiseless fall—shattered, what am
I saying? In reality, it had never existed. The earth, this
scene of a divine drama of redemption, was not situated
at the center of the universe; it was a simple little planet
that, along with its one moon, humbly revolved around
the sun, like Jupiter with its "Medici stars". A millennia-
old illusion went up in flames like a sheer curtain, and
we plunged with both eyes open—no, with everything
we had hitherto thought and believed—into the naked
infinitude of the universe. Suddenly Diana cried out—
was it a cry of delight or of horror? This cry could not be
forced into any definition, it was quite simply the sound
of the Ineffable that we were experiencing. Immediately
thereafter, she clasped both my hands—it was the first
time we had touched each other.

"So it is true, then, my friend," she cried, beside herself, "so it is true, then! There is no room for our faith
now in the universe; nothing is left but eternal laws and
ourselves!" A moment later she fell into my arms, her
breast against mine, having fled from the infinity of space
and clinging to me. And now it suddenly seemed to me
as though the infinity of space had been transformed into
the infinity of my adoring love, as if it had exchanged its

terrifying name for a blissful one, and I had to declare my feelings, rejoicing and sobbing, for this beloved creature unto my downfall.

But Diana was already standing up straight again. She stroked her disheveled hair with both hands and looked at me with a glance that harbored something of the relentlessness of the iron laws of heaven. "Oh, my friend, my dear friend," she said solemnly, "now it is decided: the Master will be condemned, he is ruined." As she said this, she grabbed my shoulders as though trying to wake me from a dream. Slowly her words sank in, but they were completely incomprehensible to me. For had we not just recognized together with the utmost clarity the truth of the new theory about the earth and the heavens? How, then, could the Master be condemned, if this theory was the truth after all? On the contrary, I was convinced that he could never again be defeated but, rather, that his judges were already the losers. And I told her, too.

She caressed my hair and forehead affectionately, as one caresses a child, but her eyes lost nothing of their relentlessness. "Precisely because it is the truth, he will be condemned", she said very softly. "He must be condemned —did we not just discover for ourselves that there is no more room for the God of our faith in the infinity up above? Or can you imagine that God's Son came down from heaven for the creatures of our tiny orb? But the Church cannot admit this, she must not admit it, for . . ." and now she spoke more softly, almost whispering—"it is too terrible!" She shuddered with horror. "We no longer have a God who cares about us; now we have only ourselves!" And then, almost like an incantation: "Only ourselves, now, only ourselves! From now on, man must be everything for man! But what is man, and what is to become of him in the future?"

But now the horror seized me, too, and I began to dread the words of my beloved. I had come from a family of strict believers and was always pious (although now I no longer am, I can say without boasting), and it would never have occurred to me that this new theory of the world that had risen above the horizon of my science could be detrimental to the faith—indeed, even my German master had always remained a devout Christian.

"Diana," I exclaimed, beside myself, "how can you say such dreadful words? You yourself are providing reasons for the Church to condemn the Master, reasons that the Master himself never gave her. Your uncle always showed the Church that it is possible to acknowledge the new science and to be a Christian at the same time."

"The Master is deceiving himself," she insisted, "but the Church will not let herself be deceived—she must condemn the Master. There is no escape unless he recants."

I was horrified once again. "The Master will never do that", I exclaimed. "That betrayal would cost him his eternal happiness!"

She smiled mysteriously. Her eyes, opened wide by the magnitude of the insight, were deep blue like the flood tide of the heavenly expanse. "There is no more eternal happiness, my little friend," she breathed, "but there is no more hellfire, either—now there is only the fire with which they burned Giordano Bruno."

My horror now knew no bounds, for women often

have premonitions that come true, do they not? Was it not said of old that they can tell the future? O God, if I had not loved and adored her so unutterably, I would have fled from her now, I was so frightened by her unbelief. But naturally I could not flee from her; even the utmost dread could not extinguish the enchantment of being close to her. That surge of horror immediately sank back into delight, like streams of water disappearing into a conflagration.

Meanwhile she looked at me attentively, with remarkable understanding. "Do you really love me, my little friend?" she asked.

She did not know the answer?! "May I love you, then?" I cried, trembling.

She replied: "Yes, you may, I need your love very much. Love me, please, love me!" She threw herself again into my arms. And now I knew nothing more of the horror that she had just instilled in me, and I closed my own mouth, which tried to say no, by kissing her again and again. So we remained for a long time in silence: the narrow attic room, "the Gate of Heaven", now had really become the gate of heaven for me.

Several days later, the lightning from Rome struck as Diana had foretold. I was just strolling with the Master's other students—young noblemen from many different lands—in the garden of the venerable Master's villa, for we had unanimously decided to wait there for his imminent return, which we did not doubt. Suddenly we saw a coach swaying through the garden gate; it stopped in front of the villa, and two older ladies and a young priest climbed out of it. Whereas the former inquired about Lady Adriana, the Master's sister, the cleric approached us and asked in a guarded, courteous tone whether he was speaking to the Master's students. Then he briefly and discreetly informed us that his Lord—he named the Cardinal whom we customarily described as the Master's patron and protector—had instructed him to convey to us the advice, not to mention the command, that we should disband quietly as soon as possible and make sure that each of us returned to his native land and his family. Of course we were profoundly shaken by this message, for it plainly implied the certainty that our Master's case was not going well—and in fact, he had already been brought to the Palace of the Inquisition. At first we stood there, as though thunderstruck; then we began to besiege the young cleric with questions. But now his face assumed an expression of completely inaccessible reserve: he pointed out to us curtly, in stern words, that no information whatsoever is given about the workings and decisions of the Holy Office—we ourselves knew all too well that that was the case. Precisely this impenetrable silence about ongoing trials was the thing about the Inquisition that instilled such fear.

While we stood there in horrified silence, Diana appeared at the door of the villa and waved to me. "My friend," she said with composure, "now it has come to what I told you: the Master is in the hands of the Inquisition. The Cardinal has advised you and your fellow students to flee; obey him, so that you may salvage the Master's work. They are summoning me to Rome; we must part."

At her words I paled: the Cardinal was summoning Diana to Rome—what did that mean? Why were there different instructions for her than for us, the Master's students, whom they were plainly trying to shield from the indictment by sending us home? Was the summons to Rome a subpoena of Diana? Had she, too, been indicted, and would she, like the Master, have to justify herself before the ecclesiastical court? She guessed my thoughts and shook her head: "No, on the contrary," she said, "the same command was issued to me as to you: I have been called back to my family and my native land."

"To your family and your native land?" I repeated uncomprehendingly. "Are you then not the Master's niece and at home with him?" She shook her head again, but at the same time placed her finger on her lips, for now the voices of the strange ladies could be heard from inside the villa. Lady Adriana came and bade Diana to be so good as to help her pack her things, since the ladies wanted to depart with her in an hour. She replied that she would be right there, and then—once again left alone with me—she repeated her demand: I must flee abroad and salvage the Master's work.

"And you?" I asked, "what will become of you?"

"I will stay by our Master, and if worse comes to worst, I am determined to share his fate", she said.

"Then you have been denounced to the Inquisition?" I blurted out.

She replied, "No, on the contrary, the Cardinal will protect me from it, but he can protect you only if you obey him. Adieu, my little friend, we must part."

But now I rebelled: "No, I am not leaving you", I said.

"Did you not allow me to love you? Did you yourself not ask me to do so, and if it was only out of despair and loneliness that you threw yourself into my arms—what does that matter to me? I love you! If you want to share the Master's fate, I want to share yours."

She could no longer reply, because Lady Adriana had already come back to urge her to make haste. She followed her into the house, while I, too, for my part set about making preparations for the departure.

When the two ladies boarded the carriage with Diana an hour later, my servant and I were already seated on our horses and ready to follow the coach. But now a conflict arose. The two ladies whispered with the priest, whereupon he walked over to me and politely but very definitely told me that I should follow the Cardinal's orders and return to my native land. In vain did I argue that if my servant and I accompanied them, it would mean protection for the traveling women. To put an end to the quarrel, I decided to let the coach ride off alone but then to follow it at some distance. Of course, my ruse was detected at the border of the papal states, where we had to change horses and show our passports. And now the indignation of the traveling party at my disobedience knew no bounds. Naturally a thousand questions burned in my soul, but whenever I tried to get near Diana during our stop at the border station, the two ladies fluttered around her like excited hens protecting their chick from danger, while the young priest punished me by ignoring me completely. Meanwhile, I indulged in extremely impious wishes: a holdup by the bandits of the papal states, broken wagon wheels, the wild animals of the Campagna

—anything would have suited me if it only gave me the opportunity to protect Diana; indeed, my young blood reveled in such conceits.

And in fact, we had crossed the border of the papal states and gone only a few miles farther when I noticed that the sound of the wheels of the coach, which had disappeared around a corner of the woods, suddenly fell silent. In its place, a wild commotion arose and frightened cries for help. My servant and I set spurs to our horses, and as we galloped around the corner of the woods, we saw several audacious oafs who had already hauled the baggage down from the wagon and forced the travelers to get out. We fired our pistols, and immediately the rabble disappeared into the thickets of the forest, as though the earth had swallowed them up. While my servant and the coachman loaded the ladies' baggage again, I finally succeeded in speaking to Diana for a moment undisturbed. "I knew you would follow me," she said, "and I was very frightened for you, but this raid was a bit of unexpected good fortune. After this incident, the Cardinal will welcome you most graciously and try to protect you, for he loves me very much: tell him everything you said to me at the Gate of Heaven. Convince him that one can affirm this theory of the world and yet be loyal to the Church— you can do the Master no greater service, and in any case you will save yourself. And let it not vex you if we must be apart at first in Rome: the important thing is that you speak, not to me, but to the Cardinal."

During the rest of the journey, both the two ladies and the young priest behaved toward me in a completely different way; they did not grow weary of praising God's

Providence, which sent me to help in the nick of time. The young priest, however, offered not only to arrange suitable lodgings for me in Rome, but also to introduce me to his Lord, the Cardinal, who would make it a point to thank me for the protection I had accorded to Lady Diana. So we arrived in Rome on the best of terms.

Now at first we spent a few days waiting, which I employed to become acquainted with the Eternal City. All of Rome was then filled by the fantastic arrival of the new Polish ambassador to the Holy See. Everyone was talking about the gold-shod hooves of his Arabian horses, the silver armor of their riders, and their richly embroidered caparisons—I could not marvel enough at the extent of the curiosity and worldly show in the Eternal City. I learned also from the ambassador of my sovereign, to whom I introduced myself immediately, that the cardinals earned a reputation for themselves by organizing magnificent theater productions and operas—in short, this Rome, which I had imagined in the somber splendor of zeal for the faith, surged with all the beauty and joyfulness of the world. Everywhere stylish palaces were being built, for which the remains of the old palaces and public baths were plundered. The common folk stood and gaped at it all and seemed to enjoy it. I also saw enchanting fountains with stone creatures from the pagan era, which plunged with their conch-shell horns into the foaming water, while live little boys rode jubilantly on the backs of marble dolphins. Then again I was captivated by the proud cavalcades of the papal nobility, especially those of the nephews of the reigning pope, who, as someone told me, were, after him, the mightiest lords in Rome. Now for me, who came from poor Germany, which was torn by decades of religious war, this extravagance appeared at first somewhat repugnant, especially when I perceived that no one here inquired about the bitter sufferings of my native land. Even the young priest of my traveling party, who as the Cardinal's house chaplain had meanwhile introduced me and was arranging my audience with him, listened only distractedly when I spoke to him about the great German war. Nevertheless, the general state of cheerful worldliness here was in a certain way reassuring to me, after all, when I thought about my Master's fate; for could a Rome that was so involved in festivities and pomp really take the Inquisition as seriously as I had been informed?

Meanwhile, the young priest had kept his word: after a few days I received the promised invitation that summoned me to His Eminence. I was prepared to meet a merry band of singers and actors in his palace, but now that was not the case. The rooms through which I was led were austere and solitary—they had that air of mourning and renunciation that I remembered from the residences of high-ranking princes of the Church in my homeland that my father had visited, now and then accompanied by me. Finally, I was brought into a chamber that was crammed with a wide variety of instruments with which I was very well acquainted. Even a globe stood on the table; maps on which the constellations were drawn lay spread out next to it—there could be no doubt that the occupant of this room was very closely associated with my own science.

Then the Cardinal entered. Now he was, as I had expected, a great lord from head to toe, with a bold, reticent countenance. His beard, which according to the custom of our time was trimmed to a point, gave him a somewhat worldly aspect that reminded me of the generals of the great German war. Yet to me this was not the most surprising impression made by his appearance; rather it was a similarity in his eyes and forehead that startled me so much I could scarcely keep my composure. Had I seen Diana again unexpectedly, I would not have been more perplexed.

After holding out his hand to me so that I could kiss his ring, the Cardinal spoke to me in the lively, amiable way of a man of the world. By right he ought to be angry with me, he said, because I had thrown his well-intentioned advice to the winds and, instead of returning to my native land, had set out for Rome. Nevertheless, the thanks he owed me for protecting his niece were the most important thing, and he did not want to withhold them from me—indeed, sometimes heaven can make use of an act of disobedience, too, in order to arrive at its destination, and he wished to show no less magnanimity. As he mentioned his niece, a very soft, indeed, tender expression flitted over the prelate's features, which detracted slightly from the serenity of the cleric but made the man that much more attractive.

Nonetheless, he continued, the apprehension that had prompted him to insist on my departure was not dispelled, and now that I was in Rome, there was no other possible way to avoid certain difficulties that threatened me, the well-known student of my Master, than to take refuge in his, the Cardinal's house. He hoped that it would not displease me to play the role of his secretary for a while, for I had probably gathered already from the furnishings of this room that his niece's love of the stars was inherited from her family. Once again during those last words, a very human trait of tenderness flitted over the prelate's features. He himself, he concluded, would enjoy my presence, because he had ascertained that I was also the student of a highly renowned German master, about whom he would gladly have a more detailed report.

This last remark made me prick up my ears, for did it not reveal that the Cardinal was closely associated also with the ideas of my present Master? He seemed to read this opinion from my expression, for he suddenly said with no introduction whatsoever: "Yes, those are great hypotheses, my young friend, very bold hypotheses . . ." It was as if he intended with that last remark to show me the path I should take with my own words. Right after that, however, he engaged me in such a stimulating conversation about these hypotheses that I was inclined to think he was just as convinced of my Master's truth as I myself was.

And so I was now welcomed into the Cardinal's household, and as I had previously worked with my Master's equipment, so now I worked with his; I had unlimited authority to use them and, what was even more significant, unlimited authority to record the results of my observations and occasionally to present them to the Cardinal. In so doing, I soon found that I was allowed to speak with the utmost candor about my Master's science. The Cardinal actually insisted on this candor: he listened to me without contradiction, indeed, he occasionally made a remark that facetiously agreed with my arguments, for instance: Perhaps it would be very salutary for proud humanity to consider for once that its earth is not the center of the universe but merely one very poor little planet. And although from time to time he also repeatedly interpolated his remark about the great hypotheses into our conversation, as a sort of warning signal, yet he never opposed my train of thought. However, as soon as I tried to turn the topic from my Master's science to his fate, he immediately interrupted me, and although in his aristocratic way as a man of the world he never insulted me with a command to be silent, he still let me sense very clearly that here lay the boundary I was not allowed to overstep.

Meanwhile, I saw and heard nothing of Diana, and although I wished to pay my respects to her and her two traveling companions, the Cardinal's chaplain discreetly but definitely opposed that wish by pointing out to me that I was not allowed to take a single step outside the palace of His Eminence. Slowly it became clear to me: I was in a sort of captivity, perhaps even in a prison superintended by the Inquisition, and probably Diana, too, being a student of the Master, was similarly confined, although through the Cardinal's magnanimity we were being held, so to speak, under house arrest. Even though I was forbidden to go out, within the palace I had the utmost freedom to allow myself to be seen and to move about without constraints. Every day I attended the early Mass that the Cardinal celebrated in his house chapel in the presence of all sorts of aristocratic personages from the neighboring palaces; many times I was ordered to dine at his table, where then the conversation among his guests very often quickly turned to my science, and I discovered to my increasing amazement that my Master had numerous well-wishers among the high-ranking clergy of Rome. In fact, I could scarcely imagine that there was an Inquisition in this enlightened and noble Roman society, and when I recalled the fate of Giordano Bruno, which Diana had conjured up at the Gate of Heaven, it seemed to me just like a fairy tale. Of course, at the table of His Eminence they did not fail to mention the misgivings on the part of the Church about the discoveries of the new science, but I welcomed these objections, for they gave me an opportunity to argue zealously that one truth cannot possibly contradict another. Indeed, I let myself get carried away and passionately assured my fellow guests that through the newly discovered theory of the heavens God the Creator was now revealing himself even more gloriously. They listened to me, silently, yet, as I supposed, not without goodwill. And in my youthful inexperience I did not suspect that these table talks were a sort of hearing, but instead I unreservedly indulged in the joyful awareness that I was coming to the aid of my venerable Master and at the same time earning Diana's praise. Yes, this thought lent a secret magic to all those discussions and brought about in my young heart a mystical fulfillment of its innocent love, so that the outward separation from the one whom I adored was repeatedly overcome inwardly. The Cardinal, too, was included to a great extent in this hidden magic:

I now knew that Diana was the child of his sister, the one female creature whom he had unreservedly honored and loved and whom he now continued to love in her daughter. He did not want to practice nepotism like the other cardinals, and he did not parade before the eyes of the world the tender, paternal love he felt for this niece —it had never misled him into ambitious marriage plans for her. With understanding he had unselfishly given in to the pressure of her "love of the stars", as he put it, and entrusted her to the Master, albeit disguised by the pretense that she was a close relative of his.

But I should return to the mealtime conversations of my host. One day, when I was once again ordered to dine at the Cardinal's table, I noticed among the guests—they were all high-ranking prelates—one almost wretchedly attired, extremely ascetical-looking priest. I took him for one of those very poor clerics without a benefice with which Rome was swarming and supposed that the Cardinal had invited him out of pity. He ate his meal quietly and did not say a word during the conversation at table, which had again turned to the familiar topic. Yet it struck me that today a somewhat different mood prevailed than on other occasions—a slight uneasiness, the cause of which was obscure to me.

"Well," one of the prelates said to me, "I concur with you that belief in the Creator may gain even greater majesty and glory as a result of the new theory of the universe. But what about the redemption? Is it conceivable that God would send his only begotten Son to this poor little planet Earth of your Master's teaching?"

I replied: "In the redemption, God reveals himself in man; faith in redemption can never be shaken by considerations about the heavenly bodies; it can be shaken only if man fails."

At these words the silent ascetic raised his head: "You are right about that, young man," he said, "yet man is weak—he ought not to venture to question God about mysteries that his wisdom has concealed from us." He said this in a soft, downright frail voice, yet everyone else instantly stopped speaking; it was almost as though they were holding their breath.

"We do not question God", I replied. "We question nature."

"Nature", the ascetic countered, "is a pagan woman. The great master Aristotle knew how to deal with her. We have reason to be grateful to him, for where would we be if everyone wanted to venture to explore on his own?! Someone once independently questioned the Bible a hundred years ago, and the division of the Church resulted from it. In the present case, I fear, now a division between God's world and man's world will result. Young man, do you never fear that you are being deceived?"

I replied: "Our equipment and instruments are honest, they do not betray us, they have neither fear nor ambition, and they speak the truth."

"But their answers contradict Sacred Scripture", the ascetic made himself heard. "It says in the Bible: 'Let the sun stand still over the valley of Gibeon', and not 'Let the earth stand still.'"

"How that is intended, I do not understand", I said honestly. "The Bible is not a textbook of natural science.

I know that God is and remains the Lord of creation, regardless of how much I may or may not know about it."

"Bravo", the Cardinal exclaimed. "The new theory of the universe will not be dangerous for young people of this sort!" As he spoke these words, he turned to the ascetic.

"And even if it were dangerous for them at first," I exclaimed passionately, "should not the truth be honored nevertheless?"

Now the Cardinal drew back. "Yes, that is precisely the big question," he said hesitantly, "but now it is presented a little differently: Can something be truth if it contradicts the faith?"

I was about to reply: "Can something contradict the faith if it is the truth?" But now the ascetic interfered again: "Holy Church determines what truth is", he said, looking intently at me, whereupon I said nothing and the whole company respectfully fell silent.

In the evening of that same day, the Cardinal's young chaplain challenged me: "Do you know that today you stood, so to speak, before the Inquisition?" he asked. "The silent guest was none other than the Censor of the Holy Office."

"Have I harmed the Master?" I asked, startled.

He placed a finger at his lips, but it seemed to me that he looked quite confident.

A glimmer of hope appeared at that time, too, that I might see Diana again. One day at the early Mass in the Cardinal's chapel, I noticed Diana's two traveling companions. I approached them after the conclusion of the liturgy, and our greeting left no doubt that they were still very well disposed toward me. Eagerly nodding, so that their black lace veils moved vigorously, they whispered to me that Diana was safe and sound, staying with them, although in deep seclusion; nevertheless, the mystery surrounding their guest would shortly be revealed, namely, when a certain plan of the Cardinal became ripe for discussion. Then they introduced me to a young French marquis as their relative, whereby they did not forget to extol me as the guardian of their journey, and then the young Frenchman extended his hand to me somewhat condescendingly. As indefinite as these hints by the ladies were, they nevertheless stirred up my hopeful expectations, and soon enough the riddle would be solved as well.

A few days later, when I had once again been commanded to appear at table in the evening, I found the Cardinal on the balcony, where he had set up the telescope for the Marquis. As I entered, he greeted me with the words: "We are celebrating today the betrothal of my niece, and therefore we are having a little party, which you, dear friend, must not miss, since we owe it largely to you that we can celebrate it in the first place." As he said these words, which obviously referred to my role as guardian, he turned to the Marquis, who again in his somewhat haughty manner offered me his hand.

Now, God knows, I had never imagined that I had any right to my beloved, much less ever thought that I might take her as my wife. I could not picture my starry queen, my Urania, as I called her in my boyish infatuation, as a married woman at all. The announcement by His Eminence struck me like a thunderbolt—in vain I struggled for the words they were obviously expecting from me. But the door had already opened, and Diana came in, led by the two ladies, her traveling attendants. She wore, as they did, the beautiful court-dress that Roman protocol prescribed for women and the black lace veil, beneath which her face appeared narrow, pale, and passionately agitated. The Cardinal walked over to her, clasped her hand, and led her with a paternal gesture toward the Marquis: "Here, my dear niece," he said, "is the husband I have arranged for you. May your future tie of matrimony be blessed."

But now something unexpected, indeed, unprecedented happened: Diana, who upon hearing the Cardinal's words had turned extremely pale, drew her hand back. "Your Eminence," she said with a gesture that expressed pride, dignity, and the relentlessness that I still recognized from the Gate of Heaven, "I cannot consent to your choice, for I have already chosen my destiny—there is only one man on earth whom I would follow to the end of the earth—even if it be to imprisonment and death." I do not know whether she really spoke those last words or whether within my own soul I caught them from the depths of hers; I just know that something like scales fell from my eyes: she loved the Master—who was imprisoned and perhaps in danger of death! And immediately it was as though I had always known that she loved him and him alone and that this was the indescribable magic of her whole being, which my love had felt like the fragrance of one and the same flower that bloomed in the depths of both our lives.

Meanwhile, we all stood there as though paralyzed by

Diana's refusal, and then the Cardinal, controlling his composure, turned urbanely to the young Frenchman: "We have frightened my niece, Lord Marquis," he said, "we have proceeded too abruptly. Excuse this man of the Church, who is ill prepared for his paternal role with regard to a young maiden."

"I ask you, on the contrary, to excuse me, Your Eminence", the Marquis replied. "I am not accustomed to playing the rejected suitor." He bowed with icy courtesy and left the room. The Cardinal gave a sign to the two visibly horrified attendants of Diana, whereupon they followed the nobleman, who was hurrying away, evidently to appease him. I expected that the Cardinal would likewise dismiss me, but he had apparently forgotten me.

"My child," he said, turning to Diana, "is it not clear to you that your position in Rome is not without danger? The Marquis wants to offer you the protection of his name and his homeland—you have just ruled out a plan for the sake of your security and future that cost me very dearly. It will not be easy to reinstate it."

"Do not reinstate it, Your Eminence," she cried passionately, "I beseech you, do not do that—it would be useless. You have no influence on my fate."

He looked at her with increasing consternation. "Do you perhaps wish to dispute my right to care for you, Diana?" he asked seriously. "Until now the daughters of Christian Rome have not insisted on choosing their husbands themselves. What brings you to this insubordination?" She gave no answer, but a strong, alarming aura proceeded from her silence. The Cardinal did not turn his gaze from her for an instant—and suddenly this gaze became strangely alert; no doubt he had understood that Diana was no longer a daughter of Christian Rome. Immediately he asked her: "Have you already seen the 'Medici stars', Diana?" Then, without waiting for her answer, he turned to the telescope that he had previously set up for the Marquis and gestured to her to come onto the balcony.

Suddenly she began to tremble. At the same time, her face again assumed that relentless expression, as before at the Gate of Heaven. A nameless fear seized me: I felt we were drawing close to an abyss; I felt Diana was capable of betraying her defection to the Cardinal. Had she gone mad? Anyone else in my place would have thought her so, but I knew better. What mattered to her was destroying every possibility of this detested marriage—she would rather fall into the hands of the Inquisition. Yet was she not aware that she thereby pronounced a sentence on her beloved Master, also? But no, she had never reckoned on his escape—oh, this unbelief of hers was much more terrible than I had suspected! She was despair itself, for renouncing faith in God, as I recognized at that moment for the first time, means abandoning the original cause of life—which means renouncing life itself.

Meanwhile, she had walked over to the telescope that the Cardinal had set up for her. Now she cast a glance into it. As she did, she trembled more and more; it was as though a noiseless storm from outer space collided with a young, already uprooted tree. She surrendered to it without resistance: slowly, almost solemnly she covered her face with her hands—a gesture of concealment that signified acknowledgment. The Cardinal had understood.

"Why do these stars frighten you, my child?" he asked gently. "Do you dread the cold endlessness of the universe? Can you no longer recognize God the Father in it, just as you no longer recognize me?"

We had reached the abyss, and in a moment it would engulf all the confidence in the Master's cause that I myself had built up in this house. And already the Cardinal was saying: "Are you then of the opinion, Diana, that the endlessness out there could swallow up the faith? Is it a universe without God that you think you see and that you profess? Is the work of your Master, then—indeed, is he himself, then, really an enemy of the Church, a justly accused man whom we would have to condemn?" It was the first time the Cardinal had ever mentioned the Master's trial in my presence. "Answer me, my child", he said. The command was not stern, yet inescapable. It suddenly occurred to me that I had heard that the Cardinal had strictly forbidden torture in the trials of the Inquisition, because the force of his personality and will alone were enough to obtain every public confession. Yet there would be no need to apply that here: Diana had no thought whatsoever of evading a confession. She stood erect as though emancipated to become a new human being.

"And if that were so, Your Eminence, if they really were to declare the Master an enemy of the Church," she said passionately, "would the Church then not have to clasp her enemy to her bosom—would she not have to love him—would this not be her only remaining alternative, the only true victory over the defection, and at the same time the only sanction by Him whose viceroy on earth she believes herself to be?"

He replied: "The Church, my child, loves even when she judges, but it is not for you to judge her."

Thereupon something like a demon came over her— an event took place that was swift as lightning yet seemed to leap over a vast expanse. Her sorrow over her loss of faith took flight into hatred of the faith. "So then, you burned Giordano Bruno at the stake out of love", she exclaimed. "Oh, then I am happy to be rid of you! Truly, the day will come when they do the same to you—the same science that you destroy will destroy you!"

At these words of hers, the Cardinal had become deathly pale. "You are right, my child," he said, "you are perfectly right: if faith in God is extinguished, the world will no longer fear anything." He hesitated for an instant. I felt that a decision was being prepared that was inevitable after what had just happened.

"Your Eminence," I said, stepping forward with my hands uplifted, "spare your niece, forgive her, if she is not yet equal to the new theory of the universe, nevertheless . . ." I wanted to say, "nevertheless she will be", but he did not allow me to pronounce the words. Instead, with an imperious hand gesture, he ordered me to be silent. No longer was he the patron of my youthful enthusiasm or the friend of my science and the affectionate guardian of Diana; he was now only a prince of the Church. "You too are right, my friend," he said calmly, "my niece is not equal to the new theory of the universe; she never will be, for it is something beyond a human being as such. Bring Lady Diana to her sedan-chair; the ladies will be expecting her." It struck me that he neither held out his ring for her to kiss nor gave her his blessing. She made no attempt to win him over; perhaps she did not even notice the lack of his favor—she was beside herself, she was exhausted to the point of swooning. She willingly let me lead her out.

As we left the palace, the sedan-chair was nowhere to be seen. I turned to the doorman and learned from him that the ladies had already gone home in the sedan-chair but had promised to send it back right away. Meanwhile, Diana had already walked farther into the courtyard, which, like all Roman courtyards, was filled with the acrid fragrance of thickly planted laurel bushes. I followed her, but not without dread: Would she not have to experience now an awakening that could only be terrifying? But my apprehension was unfounded: the face bathed in moonlight that she turned toward me bore the expression of an almost inebriated joy. "I am free, I am free", she whispered breathlessly. "I have destroyed this horrible wedding plan! The Cardinal can no longer give the heretical woman to the Marquis in marriage—this was what I wanted, this! So be glad with me, my little friend, oh, please, be glad with me!"

"I cannot be glad", I replied. "O Diana, how could you put yourself at risk in this way! I would die of fear for your sake if I did not know how much the Cardinal loves you." She did not comment on this last remark—again her inebriated glance struck me. "Do you think I would want to live in safety if the Master perishes?" she asked. I replied that I still hoped he would be set free, because of what I myself had discussed with the Cardinal concerning the new science and the inviolability of our faith. She stroked my forehead and hair affectionately, as once before at the Gate of Heaven: "So, you are still the same, my little guileless friend! But just be as you are, stay that way, only try to convince the Cardinal to spare you, because one of us must go free so as to continue the Master's work. I told you that once before. This work must never perish—your task is to carry it into the future. Promise me that you will do it!"

"I will promise anything you want, Beloved," I stammered, "but . . ."

"Why do you call me Beloved," she interrupted me, "when you know now that I belong to another?"

I replied: "I always knew that you did not belong to me, but it never prevented me from loving you . . . Can you not understand that squandering oneself in vain makes one happy?"

"Oh, yes," she said softly, "oh, yes, I understand that: after all, the Master does not love me but only his stars, and it is right for him and for me just like that. But you, my little friend, you should have a better chance!" Again she stroked my hair affectionately.

"No," I objected passionately, "it is right for me, too, just like this—I love my mysterious happiness, which is the same as yours: we two can never be disappointed."

Now she looked at me tenderly with her big eyes: "What you say is very good," she whispered, "and how badly I misunderstood you! Forgive me that I did not know you better. We are then like brother and sister because of our love—yes, certainly, we are very closely related to each other because we have squandered our hearts in the midst of all the others who will never understand us, for, oh, how coarse and dreary is the love of most people! But you are my brother . . ." She embraced me again as at the Gate of Heaven, and I, too, placed my arm around her. And now it seemed to me as though not only fraternal happiness but also a profound security with respect to any fate came over the two of us as a result of our love.

We were startled out of this intimate union when we heard footsteps approaching. A servant announced that the sedan-chair was ready and waiting. But as we walked over to it, we immediately noticed that it was not the one we had expected. "His Eminence sent his own", the servant said, while assiduously opening the door for her to get in. And now again it was as if a whole world of doom was about to tumble quite suddenly out of that little door. I felt the urgent desire to go with my beloved, yet I was forbidden to leave the palace; today, of all days, the Cardinal must not be angered even more. But the open door of the sedan-chair seemed to frighten Diana, too. "O God," she said, "it is as narrow and stifling in there as in a prison, almost like a coffin!" She literally recoiled from getting in.

I suggested: "Would you not rather wait for the sedan-chair of your attendants?" But she was already smiling again and, looking at me with that inebriated glance as before, she said quickly: "No, no, one sedan-chair or another leads to the same destination! Farewell, my little friend, and think of your task." Then she nimbly climbed in, the servant closed the door and barred it, and even before Diana could push back the closed curtain at the window so as to wave goodbye to me, the bearers, stepping double time, hurried away with the sedan-chair. An overpowering desire to see my beloved again seized me and, at the same time, an oppressive fear. "Stop! Stop!" I shouted, hurrying after the bearers, but they did not listen to me—they had already reached the exit from the courtyard, and a moment later they had disappeared.

As I returned to the palace, it was already oppressively quiet and desolate in the corridors and staircases; apparently all the occupants had just retired for the evening. There was nothing left for me but to do likewise, but first I had to perform my evening duty of closing the observatory and putting away its instruments. I entered the room through an adjoining chamber, the thick carpet of which muffled my steps. The candles in both rooms had already been extinguished; it was dark inside, and only the blue Roman moon shone in through the window and bathed with its glistening light the corners of the large, heavy pieces of furniture—they loomed out of the darkness like the peaks of mountains. The whole room seemed remarkably strange and ghostly. Entering quickly, I walked toward the balcony so as to bring in the telescope. As I reached the middle of the room, I noticed the Cardinal. He sat with his head bent over, hands covering his face, his figure and purple robe wrapped in darkness, as though he had thrown a cloak of mourning over them. The moonlight played only upon his well-formed, powerful hands, which had so often imparted blessings—it was as though they, too, were poised, like everything in the room, over a ghostly abyss.

I stopped short in alarm, and then I immediately tried to go back, but I had already been noticed. The bent-over figure lowered his hands from his face, which now revealed, as they did, a disturbing helplessness. He had the appearance of a man who after an extreme effort finally and without inhibition abandons himself to weakness. A human being should not allow himself to be seen by another in that state unless he is willing to accept unutterable pity.

"Excuse me, Your Eminence, I did not mean to startle you", I stammered. Instinctively I bent my knee—it was a protestation of my reverence, which I thought I had to pay to the bent-over figure especially in his hour of weakness. Minutes passed, in which I did not dare to move. The room increasingly assumed a strange aspect unlike its appearance by day. The Cardinal remained in the same sunken posture. Finally he made a motion: "You did not startle me," he said wearily, "I expected you: I was longing for company. Stand up and explain what brings you here." Even at the moment of his greatest weakness, his command seemed to have compelling force. Nevertheless, I was able to obey it only partially. "I ask, Your Eminence, for permission to remain on my knees", I said. "It is the appropriate posture for me, because what brings me here is hope for your clemency."

"And what do you take that to mean, my friend?" he asked.

"O Your Eminence," I cried, "you know that as well

as I. Right now your heart is asking you for clemency, just as mine is!"

"My heart", he replied, "has only to remain silent in this case and, if you will, to suffer. You are a believer, a man loyal to the Church, and must know that."

I did know it, but had he not said, "I expected you; I was longing for company"? By God, he should have some. Now I ventured everything. "Your Eminence, I love your niece", I said. "I adore her—she is the most precious thing on earth I know."

Now he straightened up for the first time, so that his face was caught even more brightly by the moonlight. "So then I have to save you, too, my poor young friend", he said. "I understand your sorrow, and I am not ashamed to tell you that I share it. But there is something greater than the sorrow of love—there is the sacrifice of what is dearest to us." In saying these words, his voice was infinitely gentle, but it seemed to me that we were meanwhile advancing into a room as cold as interstellar space.

"No, Your Eminence," I exclaimed, "there is nothing greater than love! If your niece denied her faith, she did so in order to share the Master's fate—acquit him, and she will find her way back to the faith, for the Master himself, Your Eminence, never fell away from the faith. Trust what I say, I beg you, trust me!"

He did not object. "Why should I not trust you," he said calmly, "you are altogether trustworthy. I do not hesitate to say that you would make a splendid priest. I am glad to be acquainted with you, but it would be a big mistake to try to judge mankind as a whole by you. To be sure, neither the new theory of the universe nor the new inquiry into nature can harm the true believer—but then who believes truly?"

"You, Your Eminence", I replied boldly.

Now he made a motion that almost resembled a severe dismissal. Then he said, "I was appointed to protect the faithful; I have taken upon myself the responsibility to suppress whatever might harm them."

"Can anyone defend the faith by suppressing dangers?" I asked in return.

"You take me for a man of little faith", he replied tranquilly. "You do so because I cannot summon the confidence that Christendom is able to bear the new theory of the universe and the new science."

I ventured no answer, but even silence is one. The Cardinal understood it instantly. "To be sure," he said, "I am a man of little faith—we priests have always been men of little faith, as you use the expression, for we have always persecuted heretics and wiped them out. We have done this, even though our Lord and Master commanded us to let the weeds and the wheat grow together until the day of harvest. We have never obeyed that command; we could not obey it, because the weeds would long since have choked the wheat. Even today we will not be able to obey it."

At these last words I fell again on my knees. Once again he made a motion of severe dismissal. "Stand up", he said impatiently. "Your Master does not need your intercession: inwardly I have long since acquitted him. Yet there are men who, while themselves unassailable, are nevertheless vessels of dangerous temptation. Be certain of this: others will follow these Medici stars—dreadful constellations are in the ascendant over mankind . . ." At these last words, his eyes had opened wide; in the moonlight they appeared almost white, as though a ghostly light were illuminating them—I had the impression that a visionary insight came over him. And then he continued softly but with determination: "Just now I have seen the future of mankind—just as this unfortunate maiden conjured up her own destruction, so too mankind will one day conjure up the destruction of the world, for knowledge is always repaid with death. So it was already in Paradise with the first human beings, and so it will always be."

"And nevertheless, you yourself are a man of the future, dearest Eminence," I said, "for you, too, have accepted the new theory of the universe." He did not contradict me—it was the hour when man was laid completely bare to man. Every barrier of rank or age between us had fallen.

"Certainly," he said, "I have accepted the new theory of the universe, but do you think it holds no danger for me? What do you laymen know about us priests? What do you imagine us to be? Do you have any insight whatsoever into the abysmal temptations to which those invested with spiritual authority are exposed? Do you have even the slightest inkling of the battles we have to fight in utter, deathly solitude, without the encouragement of authoritative assurances and consolations that you are accustomed to receiving from us? Do you think, perhaps, we get along without the torments of doubt? Truly, it did not take the new science to teach us that! I assure you, not only the victims of the Inquisition are martyrs;

so are we who sentence them! For it is difficult to prepare a place for otherworldly things on earth, to make
the supernatural and invisible a certainty! Revelation goes
back much more than a thousand years, and what is the
significance of the meager miracles and spiritual gifts that
have been granted to us since? Who is to say that even
these, too, are not based on pious illusions? Or are we
ourselves—I mean the figures of the visible Church—
an irrefutable testimony? Are you acquainted with the
history of the Church? Do you know the reasons for the
schism? What do you think about the pomp and splendor
of Rome today? Do you really have the impression that
Christ's kingdom continues here? Are we not entangled
in all the affairs of this world? Is there any recondite po-
litical business in which we do not have a hand—perhaps
even must have a hand? To be sure, here there are holy
monasteries where poverty and self-denial flourish, and
there we find an Oratory of Divine Love, while in the
midst of the world there are hidden souls practicing purity
of heart—but are they not all like shipwrecked castaways
clinging to a single plank in the middle of the desolate
sea of this world—are they not like Peter, who tried to
walk on the waves and sank?"

While he said all this in a low, monotonous voice, I
had the impression that with each word he was moving
farther away from me, as though he, too, were walking
on unfathomable waters, his form and mind discolored
beyond recognition by the ghostly light of the moon, and
I was pursuing him over the abysses of the night—and yet
was not the night, too, with its strange light, sheer reality?
Now, finally, the Cardinal fell silent. He had reached the

heights of midnight and remained, so to speak, standing on its summit.

"But Peter did not sink as he was walking on the water", I said. "Instead, he grasped Christ's hand."

He looked almost angrily at me, and then, again in a low, monotonous voice: "And how, do you suppose, are we to grasp Christ's hand? Where is this hand in our present moment?" His eye was fixed steadfastly on me —again his prohibition against torture occurred to me, and I sensed his inner power to obtain confessions. At the same time, it seemed to me that, under his gaze, certainties opened up within me to which I had previously not even recognized the doors.

"Do you not think it possible, Your Eminence," I said, "that we should quite simply leave the fate of the faith to God? Even if the dangers of the world threaten to engulf it?"

"And how", he objected, "do you picture this act of leaving the faith to God—I mean, in the case under consideration?"

"If you hold back the arm of the Inquisition and set the Master free, if you pardon your niece, then this will be a complete victory for the faith—and at the same time a victory for the new truth that you yourself profess."

A long, heavy silence followed. His face, which previously had been almost unrecognizable from the afflictions of the night, slowly regained clarity. Now the sorrow therein seemed completely extinguished—blank, strange, and infinitely lonely, it was almost like the lunar landscape above in the sky—I had the feeling I could achieve no more. "May it please Your Eminence", I implored him, "to answer just one more question for me: Can you suppose, no, can you even bear the thought that the faith will be saved by a patent falsehood?"

Again, a long silence followed. Would I receive no answer? Involuntarily I closed my eyes to shut out that possibility. When I opened them again, the Cardinal had left the room.

In vain I hoped during the next two days to continue our interrupted conversation. Although in my heart of hearts I knew very well that would not happen, I was too young to resign myself to a lost hope; then, too, my high opinion of the Cardinal kept resisting the idea that he could actually decide against his better knowledge. Meanwhile, I neither saw him in the observatory nor was invited by him to his table. To my question as to whether I might pay him my respects, his valet replied that His Eminence was away for important sessions. The chaplain was not to be seen, either; presumably he was accompanying his Lord. In general, the palace was strangely desolate during those days. Slowly I was overcome by the fear that a decision was being prepared in the Master's trial by the Inquisition.

Finally, on the third day, I bumped into the chaplain on the stairs. He tried to hurry past me, but I held him fast by his cassock. He looked at me sadly and dismissively. "For God's sake, what is happening to the Master?" I blurted out.

"You know I must not say anything", he replied seriously.

"Does that mean there is no hope for him?" I cried, beside myself. My distress touched his heart—alas, it was, after all, his distress, too!

"Unless he recants", he replied, sadly.

"Never! Never! That would be betrayal; that would be a bare-faced lie!" I exclaimed.

He looked at me in a strange way. "At this point, what does 'a lie' mean?" he asked gently. Then, hastily getting away from me, he added: "Then let us pray for your Master, let us pray for him." He left.

Again I was alone in the oppressively silent palace. Everything seemed to me transformed now, the observatory devastated, robbed of its significance. Even the architecture of the house spoke a different language from before. It struck me as boastful and superficial, as though the sweeping gestures of these towering pillars and staircases concealed a secret but profound insecurity that could no longer stand up to sober reality. At this point what does "a lie" mean, the young priest had said. Did he think that the truth would be condemned? That the Master would recant? I could bear it no longer; I had to know what was happening.

During the night, which I spent without sleep, a desperate plan matured in my mind. I had now found out that the Cardinal and his chaplain rode off every morning very early. And so I waited until his coach was driving away, then I stole into the chaplain's room, took a cassock from his wardrobe, and put it on. In my disguise I succeeded in slipping out of the palace unnoticed, for the servants, having become negligent because of their master's absence, lacked their usual attentiveness. From the expeditions that I had made during my first days in Rome,

I still recalled the Palace of the Inquisition. Without difficulties I arrived at my destination. Several high-ranking prelates had just arrived at the main entrance, and their sedan-chairs and coaches surrounded the gate. I mingled with their attendants and as part of that crowd made my way through a long, gloomy corridor. A still very young Dominican friar, who was plainly very excited, dashed toward us. His searching gaze passed over my escorts and to my horror came to rest on me.

"You belong to the retinue of the Archbishop of . . .", he mentioned a name completely unfamiliar to me. "Please follow me into the gallery to the left." He did not wait for my answer but once again marched double time farther down the gloomy corridor, at the end of which a door opened and allowed me to enter. "You know your mission", he said. I had no idea what he meant, but he had already closed the door again behind him.

I found myself in a small, narrow room, which had a little glass window. I stepped up to it, pushed it back, and looked into a room that resembled a hall, in which the ecclesiastical court was just assembling in a solemn session. I saw a long table covered with black cloth, on which stood a crucifix—two candles burned on either side, yet they did not brighten the room, it seemed to me, but rather shed a gloomy light.

The judges now took their places in profound silence at the side of the table facing me, so that I could recognize their faces—these prelates were mainly the regular guests at the Cardinal's table. Then he, too, came in and sat down on a somewhat raised, pew-like seat in the middle of the table. The Censor of the Holy Office was not there; I got the impression that the Cardinal had taken the place of the absent official, so as to conduct the proceedings. Contrary to any reasonable expectation, a desperate hope awakened in me that he had appointed himself the deliverer of my Master.

Two Dominican friars, who likewise held burning candles in their hands, now led the venerable man in and accompanied him to the middle of the side of the table that had remained empty, so that he came to stand in front of the crucifix, eye to eye with the Cardinal. The gloomy light of the smoldering candles fell directly upon the latter's face, which was solemn, inscrutable, and peculiarly detached, as at the end of our conversation by moonlight.

I had been able to glimpse my Master's face for only a moment as he was coming in; now he stood with his back to my gallery—it pained me to see that he was trembling.

Meanwhile, the session had begun. A prayer was recited, invoking the Holy Spirit. Then a Dominican friar stood up at the other end of the table and began to read a Latin document aloud. It presented the Master's teaching, or, rather, the condemnation of this teaching. "Heresy, heresy", this oft-repeated word struck my ear with relentless clarity. Finally the lector fell silent. The opinions of the individual judges now followed, which were more muffled than carried by the uncanny silence in the room. The dreadful term "anathema" passed from the lips of one to the next, not fulminating majestically or angrily, but indifferently, softly, coolly, like the murmuring of an ocean wave that rolled in slowly and washed over them one by one, as though they were cold, senseless gravel on the shore. Now the wave had glided right up to the

Cardinal, and it would soon have to break. Again, contrary to any reasonable expectation, this desperate hope crept up on me! For after all, here was the one man who had acknowledged the truth of the Master's teaching, the one man who towered over the limitations of the age and could command its blindness—the one man who like Peter walked on the sea.

But the incomprehensible had already occurred: the wave had glided away over the Cardinal, too. The same voice that had admitted to me a few nights earlier that the Master's truth was convincing to him now had pronounced the "anathema" on him. Peter, walking on the sea of the blindness of the age, had sunk into it. Helplessly I clenched my fist: cursed is he who relies on men! The whole room appeared to me now like one desolate seascape of betrayal—the only thing still standing upright was the tall crucifix, but no one wanted to embrace it. And now, surely, the moment had come of which Diana had been thinking when she spoke about the fire with which they had burned Giordano Bruno, for now the sentence would be passed.

Then again a voice broke the cruel silence in the room: they were offering the accused a reprieve; they were asking whether he was willing to recant. It was of course a mere formality.

During the condemnation of his teaching, the Master had sagged more and more, but at the word "recant" he stood up straight—was it indignation? Alas, it could only be indignation—what a terrible thought, that he would annihilate his truth and his life's work!

And now I must bear the momentous, painful witness

against my master that until now has been withheld from the world for good reasons. For it was not as they tried to make the gullible world believe; the venerable man, facing death, did not renounce his truth in fear and trembling and thereby personally make a profoundly shameful confession of his error. Rather, the Master recanted in triumph, and there was not one person in the whole auditorium who did not understand that in this case a man was unwilling to do his judges the honor of refuting them, but instead, so to speak, was repaying their betrayal of the truth with his own. Was this still the same man whom I had seen trembling at his entrance into the hall? Or were these two men in some mysterious way related to each other—did the one beget the other, when they were driven to extremes? And where was the pious, loyal man of the Church whom I had so often commended to the Cardinal? Had he, too, when subjected to extreme conditions, been transformed into his opposite and fled to the other limit of his potential? All I know is this: I saw a man shrug off his own person as though it were a piece of insignificant material. There was something incredibly magnificent in his recantation: his absolute contempt for his judges was part of it, but also his contempt for himself, and this was precisely what gave his recantation its disturbing, indeed, horrible grandeur. Oh, what scorn for his own self-destruction! He allowed the man within him to fall entirely, but over that fallen man rose up the pride of the scientist, immeasurably to the point of genuinely glorious presumption. Did he express it in speech? Oh, no, he said nothing aloud, but they understood all too well what he meant to say. He meant to say: Yes, now

I am doing the same thing you did: I am betraying what I hold to be true, I am betraying my science, but you give me the freedom that allows me so easily to betray it! I know that at this moment I am unspeakably petty, but my science is great and glorious! Whether or not you condemn it and whether or not I renounce it, either way it makes no difference—this science is inviolable and unstoppable. Suffocate me here in my disgrace—I gladly choke on it, for my science will be the victor of the future!

And how did the judges now receive this most ambiguous of all recantations? Alas, for me there was only one judge there! For what did I know, after all, about the participants in the table conversations in the Cardinal's palace who had assembled here? At what final conclusion had they arrived or not arrived? The Cardinal alone stood clearly before my eyes—as though still bathed in the ghostly moonlight of our nocturnal conversation. I saw him, while the Master was recanting, sway in his elevated pew; I saw him grow pale in his purple robes. Was that vision of the future perhaps reappearing, the man of the future? Indeed, maybe that man stood before him, having become preternaturally present just because they were trying to destroy him. And now this very man had to be pardoned by him.

The Cardinal stood up, laboriously, as though he had aged many years, resembling the Master in a disturbing way: two men who had subdued the man within them stood facing each other. Was it really the Cardinal who now began to speak? Were we not still hearing, after all, the voice of the other man? Did not every one of his words tremble with the same resistance to the meaning of the words as before in the Master's recantation? They spoke of mercy, but they meant profound mistrust; they promised clemency, but how unutterably miserable it turned out to be. Instead of the stake, lifelong surveillance! The two candles on the judges' table had burned far down and now slowly went out. It went dark in the lightless room, the curtain fell. It seemed to me as though I heard the clocks of future centuries strike the hour. Two doors, which until then had stood open to each other, closed. Two intellectual chambers quaked and parted—forever—within me as well.

I then left the Palace of the Inquisition as though in flight, overcome with sorrow and loathing, disappointed in everything I had trusted and honored. In the immense collapse of my former youthful world, only one thing stood unshaken: the repudiated truth. I loved it with spite and jubilation, precisely on account of the fact that it was repudiated. Never, never would I set foot again in the palace of the Cardinal who had abandoned it! But nevermore could my place be again at the Master's side, even if the Inquisition had set him free. Once a man had renounced his truth, even if triumphantly, could he ever worthily advocate it again? Youth makes no compromises: for me the Master was forever silenced. And now came the moment when I finally understood my beloved, who from the beginning had foreseen the bad outcome but, of course, had also helped to bring it about. I wanted to devote the rest of my life to the Master's truth, as she had earnestly begged me; I wanted to lead the imprisoned

science into freedom, to salvage and continue the persecuted work—but not here, watched by the Argus-eyes
of the Inquisition. Although my German homeland was
shut off from me because of the great war, there were
other northern countries that the arm of the persecution
did not reach. Away, away from Rome! I wanted to leave
the Eternal City on that same day, because there was
no longer any place here in the future for the Master's
students, either. But was Diana not one of them? And
could it not be expected of the Cardinal that he himself
had abandoned his beloved niece, sorrowfully, but relentlessly shrugging off his heart? Certain statements during
our nocturnal conversation caused me in hindsight to
tremble. Once again I was seized with a consuming fear
for my beloved. And in any case, I had to speak to her
again, to take leave of her, to explain to her my disappearance from Rome.

With some effort I inquired about the palace of her two
hostesses and had myself announced. I was immediately
admitted, and now my worst fears were confirmed. In
tears, the ladies told me that Diana had not returned to
them on the evening when she rejected the Cardinal's plan
for her marriage. The last veil over the state of the matter
was torn: the Cardinal's sedan-chair, the closed curtains,
the departure as though in flight, my useless shouts—
O my God! What had I allowed to happen by being so
unsuspecting? Where had they taken my beloved? The
ladies had no information; the Cardinal had merely notified them that their ward was safe in a convent of the
strict observance, but accessible to no one. I understood:

discreet steps had been taken here to remove an aristocratic person who had been convicted of apostasy and at the same time to protect her from herself.

My first impulse was to storm all the convent doors in Rome, but I already sensed how childishly hopeless such an undertaking would be: the Cardinal was not one to be content with half measures: just as he demanded the ultimate sacrifice of himself, when it was a matter of safeguarding the faith, so, too, he expected it from others. I realized I was facing sheer inexorability.

So Diana's ardent wish to share her Master's fate had come true, albeit in profound, hopeless abandonment. They both now represented, so to speak, the truth that had been buried, probably forever. I pictured my beloved behind high barred windows, in silent walled gardens from which time was seemingly excluded—I saw her fade alone like a beautiful, precious flower. I knew that she could be moved by no other encouragement than by the consolation of her own strong soul, in that outwardly faceless yet inwardly deep fellowship with her beloved, a willing sacrifice to him without reward or thanks. A timid, almost pious awe crept over me: No, I must not set her free, even if I could! After all, had not her love always been love unto death? I had to leave her to her destiny and achieve my own. Achieving this was the only love I could now render to her. My decision to salvage the Master's work that had been betrayed also signified the ultimate fidelity in her regard. Without hesitation I set out.

Not until I was standing directly in front of the Porta del Popolo did I notice that I was still wearing the chaplain's cassock. There was no opportunity left now to change my clothing. I perceived this false uniform as a mockery, yet did it not offer me protection, especially at this moment?

Along the way was one of the many hundred churches of Rome. Following a pious custom, I was about to go in for a moment to pray as usual for a blessing on my journey, yet my foot stopped short on the threshold: What point would there be to it now? How could I expect a blessing for myself, when they were depriving me of my science? My home was no longer the Church but, rather, the mighty new realm of the human mind, on the threshold of which I stood. And now, almost stormily, out of the collapse of my earlier life arose a new man within me, for whom there were no longer any ties but only the law of free inquiry, without otherworldly restraint—the only thing valid for me would be what science could prove. The spiritual house that I had occupied until then had been demolished, but I would build for myself and for mankind a new house, a bold, magnificent house in freedom and truth! An intoxicating enthusiasm came over me as I now walked through the Porta del Popolo, away from the splendid façades of the Roman palaces, which concealed things I found so dreadful, away from the beloved woman for whom there was now no hope, out into the wild, lonely Campagna. Dusk was just beginning to fall; soon it would be dark. I was alone with the great, unknown Nature, beset by her riddles and mysteries—I was homeless, fleeing along foreign, impassable roads, but the night wind from the immense expanse rested on my forehead like the promised kiss.

That was the end of the document. While the young doctor was reading the final pages, sirens suddenly began wailing outside. Horrified, I jumped up, but with a strong grasp he forced me back down onto my chair. "That is only the preliminary alarm; for the time being, it doesn't concern us at all." Untroubled, he read to the conclusion. Now the door flew open, and the caretaker stuck his head in: "The warning system is reporting a major air attack; today it could get dangerous for us." My young companion stood up. "What do you mean, dangerous! Usually they just fly right over us." He stretched comfortably. Then with irritating indifference, he opened the balcony door. "We mustn't miss this display." His cold-blooded attitude shocked me, yet at the same time it had a suggestive effect—I followed him, more or less calmed.

The sirens had ceased now; the city lay below us in an almost solemn stillness, wrapped deep in its protective masquerade. Over it arched the majestic cupola of the night sky; star after star glittered with inexpressible clarity. Magically, the Milky Way shimmered like a billowing silver veil. I made the heroic attempt to take my mind off things: "Like in our document, 'At the Gate of Heaven'", I said.

He looked at me sarcastically. "Right", he said. "This is what it looks like, centuries later, 'At the Gate of Heaven' —You will notice the difference right away."

Now great white bands of light raced across the heavens, as though invisible hands were probing the sky with them. "Those are searchlights; they are looking for enemy airplanes", said the young doctor. "There, now they have found their target!" Suddenly the two bands of light came together, intersected and stood still, forming a gigantic, immobile cross in the sky. And already the sirens started howling again down below—monstrously, like a beast from the abyss. At the same time there appeared in the sky several beaming pyramids of light, which slowly floated down onto the city. Now my companion's imperturbability became animated. "Those are the enemy's Christmas trees", he exclaimed. "Quickly, now, into the cellar; Christmas trees bring death!" He grabbed me by the hand and positively dragged me back into the house. "Christmas trees bring death", I repeated, reeling. "Christmas trees? What blasphemy!"

We hurried down into the cellar, where a number of people had already gathered, the caretaker's family, a few individuals from the neighborhood. I will skip over the hours that now followed; after all, I do not even know whether it was hours—mortal terror is not measured by the hands of the clock; we were outside of time. We were outside of human realms, in the hand of satanic powers. Oh, that dreadful whizzing sound of the bombs rushing down, those horrendous roaring impacts! And yet, what a sigh of relief every time, when it had not struck us! But then suddenly mad screaming by everyone, an unimaginable crash and rattling—rubble falling down, stifling clouds of dust, darkness as deep as in the grave—at just one place flickering light gleamed through a crack in the masonry. "Go out that way", shouted the voice of the young doctor over the commotion. I crawled through with the others . . . and . . . staggered back into the depths of the cellar, because all hell was blazing outside! Then someone came after me; I was grabbed, pulled, dragged along, pushed out onto the street that was swaying in a dance of flames. That, then, was the dreadful carnival for which the city had masked itself! Again I wanted to go back into the cellar, again I felt the strong, unyielding grip of my ice-cold companion. "Forward!" Desperate, but obedient like a little child with no will of my own, I ran down the roaring avenue of flames as the street burned, house by house.

And now you will ask me about the documents I had come to the city to salvage. Naturally we had taken them with us into the cellar; I remember clearly how the young doctor put the little suitcase with the family archive beside me on the floor, while I desperately held in my arms the document from which he had read aloud. I was still clutching it firmly as I crawled through the crevice in the masonry, but then, when I caught sight of the burning street—yes, then I simply threw it away, just as the other people at the time threw away their money. The firestorm whirled the leaves up into the air . . . I saw them catch fire . . . What did it matter to me? . . .

Later, too, long after we had been rescued, I felt no regret whatsoever and no surprise about it—it had happened just as I had anticipated upon my arrival in the masked city. Now came the unmasking of this horrific carnival; it had revealed the worthlessness, not only of the document but of everything that until then had provided meaning and security in my life. I felt oddly poor and bare, ruined in what I had always believed to be valid:

humanity and Christian decency, refinement and culture, class and tradition; they were all suddenly as if they had never been, or if they had ever been, they were definitively stripped of their meaning, gone, and, with them, the meaning and purpose of my existence, which until then I had lived so confidently. My own era had been wrecked. Where did I belong now?

My cousin Marianne, who with her children was staying with me for the time being, had no sympathy with me—after all, she had not gone through that night of bombing. While I mourned irretrievable losses in my unscathed rural domesticity, she, who had actually lost her house, was already dreaming about rebuilding what had been destroyed and about a thousand new purchases for her happy home—in short, she found herself convinced that soon everything would again be exactly as it had been before. Given this attitude, the only difficulty for her to deal with was the destruction of the family documents. Naturally, she was much too considerate and kind to blame me, but she simply could not get over the fact that she herself had not traveled to the city at the time in order to fetch the records. To be sure, it was some consolation to her that the family tree and the most important dates of the family history could perhaps be compiled again from old parish registers and general historical records, but for the so-called "Galileo Document" that she had treasured so highly, there were no clues left, except in the personal recollection of those who had read it attentively. Therefore she resolved to reconstruct this document, and because I myself, in my state of mind at the time, had not been paying close attention, she invited her young cousin, who had read the document to me during that night of bombing. To our utter astonishment, after the collapse of the German front that had occurred meanwhile, he had not been taken prisoner, like Marianne's husband, but had obtained a favorable job offer overseas, which assured for him the immediate continuation of his scientific research. He wrote that he would come to say goodbye to us before his departure.

So one day he stood in front of me again, with his slim, lanky form. His sharply chiseled face still bore the somewhat superior yet at the same time slightly overwrought expression that had once irritated and unsettled me so much. In the meantime, he had saved my life—I myself would never have found the courage to leave the cellar and to dash out onto the flaming street. Naturally, it was appropriate to say that to him again. He laughed unselfconsciously: "Yes, once again you will be my claim to fame," he said, "the only one I have to show for myself along these lines."

"Frankly, you act as if you were otherwise a cannibal," joked Marianne, "and yet even during the war you only worked in a laboratory."

"Well, that was in fact the den of murderers," he replied somewhat mysteriously, "but let's drop the subject . . ." He looked around in my apartment with interest: "You have kept all the old luxurious furnishings."

"Don't you find it comforting after a ruined city?" asked Marianne.

"To be honest, the ruins have their good side, too", he said. "After all, it lets fresh air into a lot of old dumps."

"Dumps?" Marianne repeated disapprovingly, "tell me, what sort of language is that?"

Now he laughed again—toward the older generation he was still the somewhat defiant man with the youthfully disrespectful manner of speaking, but I was no longer the same toward him! Was it because I had been displaced from my own era and thereby drawn closer to him? I felt his presence was somehow liberating, as if he would surely help me out today, as he had done back then on the night of the bombing—in a word, I caught wind of the new life in him.

Marianne now started to speak about the document and urged him to help us reconstruct the story from memory. "I am so glad you read it on that last night", she said. "That way you surely know how important it is."

He showed no particular enthusiasm: Yes, he had read the thing, but he did not really think it was especially important—today the Inquisition would have no reason to be excited about this master's teaching.

Marianne assumed her childishly wide-eyed expression: "What do you mean?" she asked naïvely.

"I mean, today our science could simply tell the Lord Cardinal: Your Eminence, determine the center of the universe yourself, however you like, as it befits a theologian—we scientists are not in a position to do that."

"But that is just not possible", Marianne cried indignantly. "Then whole centuries would have fought in vain!"

"They were of course right in their time," he said, obligingly, "and they did leave us some methods, too, but ultimately everything is relative . . ."

She shook her head energetically; of course she did not believe a word of it—how was she supposed to? We both had been brought up to be in awe of infallible science. She turned to me: "Come on, help me", she cried impatiently. "What this ill-mannered man says cannot be so. I think he is not taking us seriously."

"On the contrary," I said, "he may be right, Marianne; during the night of the bombing I learned that everything, I mean everything we have and are, is fleeting."

Now she was visibly upset. "But then," she said hesitantly, "then the whole trial of the Master would have been senseless, and also the fate of poor Diana and her friend . . . Then in condemning them, the Church pointlessly put herself in the wrong with such bitter consequences . . ."

But now something completely unexpected happened. "No, damn it all, there was a point to what the Church was trying to do at the time", the young doctor snapped. "I don't mean the methods of the Inquisition; I mean the Cardinal's vision—he was in fact right! That man knew human beings. Three hundred years ago, he already knew all about people today. Diana in the document could still say: Nothing is left but eternal laws and man. Today neither eternal laws nor man exists."

"But we still believe in the good, and we are Christians, after all", Marianne stammered.

"So, are we still?" he asked. "I find that interesting. No one gives any sign of it, and I thought that that had finally been made clear by this bombing war. However, it appears that the news has not yet reached you here. But just wait, they will soon outdo Hiroshima."

In the bedroom next door, one of Marianne's children began to cry bitterly—she went over to see what the matter was. The young doctor and I were alone for a few moments.

I had grasped what he meant. The word "Hiroshima" had landed in front of me like a lightning bolt. "You must not go overseas", I said. "You must not help further this terrible development!"

His young, intense face assumed an extremely knowing expression. "I see that you get it," he said, "the reason why I'm going abroad, but it's too late. And not just because I have already made a commitment. After all, what good would it do if I stayed here—then others would just answer the call. Shall I let them take my opportunities? In any case, progress goes on, and no one is able to stop it any longer."

He said that with seemingly unconcerned assurance, but it no longer fooled me. Suddenly now our relationship turned around: I felt a superiority over him that distressed me: I felt for the first time the extraordinary, almost touching discrepancy between his lack of human maturity and the scientific expertise that he no doubt possessed—I felt now that his youth was crying out— good God, I was old enough to have been his mother! And now it would be up to me to help him, except that I was at a loss.

"But if you are seeing everything in your science in a new way, does it ever occur to you that there might be a God, too?" I cried desperately.

"Yes," he replied calmly, "the idea does in fact occur to us—after a long, long time it has occurred to us again.

It has become somewhat difficult to explain the universe without a Creator, but he is rather difficult for us to grasp; we have managed for too long to get by without him—indeed, we had to—look at the lost document! You know more about God than I."

Alas, no. Neither did I know about him after all—God had played no major role in my life, and not once had I felt this as something missing. For of course we had gone to church, we had belonged to Christian associations, and we had given presents to poor people on Christmas Eve. But now even this meager relationship with God belonged on the long list of things lost on that night of bombing. I sought a reply in vain.

Meanwhile, Marianne had returned, and we started to write down a few notes about the lost document.

It was already late in the night when the young doctor finally left us. Marianne had said goodbye to him while still in the living room and had gone to look after her children, one of whom was now crying again in his sleep. In the meantime, I accompanied the guest to his car. We walked in silence across the yard. The stars shone this night, too, in sublime splendor, as once over Diana and her young friend at the Gate of Heaven—up there the span of time since then was like only a fleeting moment; up there all our interpretations and misinterpretations were no more than meteors flaring up and going out again. But here below on earth there were failures and disasters . . .

He started the motor now—in a few minutes he would be gone—what should I send with him as a last word? He had saved my life, and now he was going overseas in order to help destroy life. Did he not mirror the world, wavering between humanity and inhumanity—and was not the world's complete helplessness reflected in me?

"You are so quiet; are you still thinking about God?" he asked casually.

I had to decide to say something: "I am thinking of how Diana was once afraid at the Gate of Heaven, because God was no longer to be found in the universe, and I think that today you are afraid you could find him again."

He hesitated a moment with his answer, then suddenly he changed his tone—for the first time! Had this tone, too, been merely a sort of disguise? The last mask fell. "Yes," he said frankly, "that may be. We are afraid, because we are standing everywhere at the outermost limits, and if we were to find our way to God again, we could no longer include him in our laws of causality—then he would be a God who really had something to say. But in the meantime, we are not yet that far along, and so let us make use of our freedom."

He shook my hand as though we were comrades, then the motor revved up, and the car started to roll . . .

I watched him drive off until the last sound had died away. Yes, God must again have something to say, even to me. After all, we were confronting the same decision. What would it be?

∿